Jane's Fragile Facade

A Pride and Prejudice Variation

Jaime Marie Lang

IDLE MUSINGS PUBLISHING

Contents

Prologue

Sitting by a lovely fire, wrapped comfortably in blankets, Evaline could not help but sigh in contentment. She was still feeling worn down, and there was the occasional tickle in her throat that made her cough. But in a room full of loving people—people she was thankful had chosen not to exclude her despite only being twelve—Evaline found solace. Had she been at home, her mother would have left her alone in the schoolroom to recover from her illness. The company was a welcome reprieve from the solitude she was accustomed to.

Her mother, Mrs. Goulding, liked her home calm, quiet, and clean. As illness rarely obeyed her dictates, she preferred anyone foolish enough to become unwell to stay out of sight and preferably out of her house. Evaline had never thought to question her mother's behavior until she got to know the Bennet sisters and realized that there were other ways besides her mother's. For now, she was grateful that her mother's way of thinking allowed her to stay happily ensconced with the family at Netherfield.

Strictly speaking, Evaline was well enough to return home, but as her mother did not think to inquire about her daughter's health, Evaline felt no compulsion to go home. It did not hurt that her brother would rather stay at Netherfield with his lady love than go home. Evaline was pleased, knowing that it turned out well for both of them to be away from the rest of their family for a time.

As she glanced around the room, Evaline could not help but feel the warmth and love that exuded from the various couples. Seated near the window were Mr. and Mrs. Darcy. Despite the many things that she had surreptitiously heard through her mother's less than discreet comments, she was now quite fond of the pair. Though it was much harder to read Mr. Darcy than his vivacious wife, she now liked them both exceedingly. At the moment, they were playing chess and only occasionally contributed to the group's conversation. If she was not mistaken, Evaline believed that though they were merely playing chess, they were somehow flirting with every move on the board.

On the settee across from her, Evaline watched Mr. Bingley and Mrs. Bingley. Jane had been acting as hostess that evening and was keeping the conversation flowing, happy and light despite the Darcys' focus on their game. Though not as demonstrative as her sister Elizabeth, Jane seemed to be just as attached to her husband, Mr. Bingley. They both always seemed to find a way to touch each other when it was not strictly necessary.

He had held her hand when they stood from the dinner table, and when she put her hand on his arm, he had quickly placed his hand over her own. Evaline knew her parents would never consider showing such affection, deeming such behavior as plebeian, but the love she witnessed here made her think about her mother's expectations for her. Evaline knew that her mother wanted her to have a splendid match when she grew up. Evaline had once wanted it as well, only now her definition of splendid had changed.

Closest to Evaline, her brother and his new fiancée shared a settee. Though they held hands, no one said a thing. In fact, none of the other couples had said a thing about the new couple breaking with propriety by touching so openly.

It would be nice to always be surrounded by such warmth and consideration. Why had her mother always vehemently rejected the idea of love? Who would not want that for themselves and their children?

"Are you warm enough, Evaline?" Jane asked, pulling Evaline from her thoughts. "You are just recovering from that horrid cough. I would hate to have you catch a chill and get worse."

Smiling at the gentle concern, Evaline hurried to reassure her. "Oh, I am warm enough. In fact, I am quite comfortable. Thank you." Pursing her lips in thought, Evaline only hesitated for a moment before saying, "I wanted to express my gratitude for allowing me to join everyone this evening."

Smiling in her quiet way, Jane replied, "Think nothing of it. You are family, or soon will be after all. You are less likely to run about and break the nicknacks than Artie and Ellie, and we have them here all the time." Seeing Evaline's sudden downcast expression, Jane got up from her spot next to her husband and approached Evaline, saying softly, "What is wrong, pet? Was it something I said?"

At a loss for words, Evaline looked to her brother and was grateful when he had the courage to say, "At home, Evaline is not even allowed to attend family meals. She stays in the schoolroom unless summoned by my mother for inspection."

Reaching out, Jane smoothed an errant strand of hair from her brow. "Well, it is her loss because I have found you lovely company and have enjoyed getting to know you."

With misty eyes, Evaline smiled in response. Trying to soak up all the older sister affection that she could from the eldest Bennet sister, she replied, "I have also enjoyed getting to know you all."

"I am glad. Would you like some more tea?" Looking at Evaline's empty teacup, Jane raised her eyebrows elegantly.

Nodding gratefully, Evaline said, "Yes, thank you. I really enjoy your tea." After filling Evaline's cup, Jane saw to the others, and Evaline gratefully took a sip of the hot brew. Before Jane had reclaimed her seat, Evaline finally felt bold enough to ask what had been on her mind for a while. Clearing her throat, she said, "When I found out the other night of how Mr. Darcy and Elizabeth came together, I was stunned. You also told me how your sister Catherine ended up with an earl. That was an interesting tale, I must say. I was there for Mary's adventure with my brother Gabriel. I saw for myself how their relationship formed, but I have yet to hear of how you ended up with Mr. Bingley. I would love to hear the story, unless you think me too bold?" Looking around the room, she smiled at her brother and Mary and then realized that Mr. Darcy and Elizabeth had looked up from their game and were watching her as well.

For a moment, Jane seemed frozen, standing between the tea service and her settee, surprise written on her face. Evaline worried that she had misspoken and was about to apologize for her blunder, but noticed Elizabeth shake her head ever so subtly and decided to keep her mouth closed. Going to his wife, Mr. Bingley placed his chin on Jane's shoulder, hugging her from behind. "Why don't you tell her, love? I know not all of our tale is pleasant, but neither was Elizabeth and Darcy's."

Turning her head ever so slightly, Jane's blue eyes met her husband's, and they seemed to have a silent conversation before she turned back to Evaline and said, "I suppose tonight is the night I will tell you the story of how I lost my heart and quite happily became Mrs. Bingley." Then, accompanying him back to their seats, she leaned into her husband and began to tell her tale.

Chapter One

"YOU ARE AN ANGEL, Miss Bennet, and the London season shines brighter with you here." Though the beaming gentleman in front of Jane probably intended for his words to flatter her, she found herself fighting a shudder. "Your beauty puts all the other girls to shame. Tell me you have another set available for me." Reaching out, he gripped her gloved forearm.

Removing her arm from his grip, Jane somehow kept her serene mask in place. "I am sorry, Mr. Forsham, but you will have to give one of the other young ladies some attention." Looking around the room, Jane spotted a sweet girl she had met earlier standing by the wall, a wistful look on her face. "Why not ask Miss Florence Meriweather to dance? She appears to be free for the next set."

With a laugh, Mr. Forsham appeared to study Miss Meriweather across the room. Then, looking back at Jane, he attempted to recapture her hand while loudly proclaiming, "You are too droll, Miss Bennet. Why would I offer to dance with a mouse such as her when I can bask in the glow of a diamond, even if I am not fortunate enough to dance with you a second time?"

Keeping out of his grasp, Jane anxiously wondered how Elizabeth or Mary might handle a similar situation. She was confident that Elizabeth would use her sharp tongue as a defense. However, a remark that would indubitably sail right over his head would not free her from her supercilious partner. Mary would start quoting scripture or Fordyce. Jane's middle sister had long ago learned that most people became uncomfortable when she started spouting scripture. It had worked especially well on their father, Mr. Bennet, whose cruelty had forced them all to develop their own sort of defense mechanisms.

Jane had developed a mask of serenity. Her father's power to hurt her diminished when she learned not to flinch, causing him to abandon his efforts after only a few stinging remarks. Jane tried to see the best in people and could often do so, but the superficiality that she was encountering in London ballrooms hurt her too tender heart. Just because she could pretend she was unaffected did not mean she was not hurt, and what hurt Jane the most was people who were intentionally cruel to others.

Seeing the look on Florence's face decided it for Jane. The poor girl had clearly heard his slight, and that simply would not do. Offering a sweet smile with intentions of disarming the gentleman—if he could even be referred to as such—Jane responded to Mr. Forsham's earlier comment. "Mr. Forsham, if you are so interested in spending time in my company, perhaps we could converse until my next dance partner arrives? Shall we discuss the war on the continent? Or would you rather speak of the state of the poor and whether you feel it has had any influence in the Luddite movement?" Raising her brows in question, Jane waited for his response, knowing full well she had discomposed him.

Mr. Forsham's eyes bulged out for a moment before he clamped his mouth shut with a tilt of his head. After hesitating briefly, he composed himself and chided, "Oh Miss Bennet, you do not have to worry your lovely little head about such matters. You are not like that mouse, Miss Meriweather. While she may need to cultivate accomplishments and *learn* things, you do not. You are a diamond. Your beauty is enough to draw me in. All you need to do is grace my arm, grace any man's arm, and they will be satisfied. *I* will be satisfied." Finally capturing her hand, he patted it as one would a confused child and then said, "You are like the sun, Miss Bennet. You do not need to worry about filling your head; you only need to shine."

Tugging her hand from his grip as delicately as possible, Jane used her sweetest voice to say, "Oh, but Mr. Forsham, have you not heard the story of Icarus? There is danger in drawing too close to the sun. Do not forget the sun will burn you if you are not careful. It may be wise to use better discretion." Dipping into a sharp curtsey, Jane bid him goodbye and stalked elegantly across the room. Those who did not truly know her would be blissfully unaware of how upset she actually was. Jane's serene beauty and tranquil demeanor had become renowned during her London season, but she had to admit to herself that her well of calm was running dry. It was becoming harder and harder for her to remain composed when presented with so many uncaring fools.

Not worry her lovely little head indeed. Jane was not stupid. She knew her looks were what people first noticed about her, but she was more than a pretty face. Making her way to Miss Meriweather, she tried to cheer up the younger girl, but quickly realized that she was not receptive to Jane's overtures of friendship. That was the second lesson she had learned in London—not all the women she met wanted to become friends with the season's brightest diamond.

She had recently overheard a conversation of two debutantes saying that having Jane Bennet stand next to you was to cast a shadow on your own beauty. No one wanted to be compared with an incomparable beauty, not that anyone would blame the superficial and empty-headed gentlemen who wanted an equally empty-headed beauty on their arm. Resigned, Jane complimented the girl's dress and moved along to find her party.

"MEN SWARM AROUND YOUR daughter like bees to honey. They seem to be unable to resist her magnetic presence," Lady Derby murmured to her companion as they watched the young blonde speak with a gentleman across the room. Cousin to Mrs. Gardiner, the countess had long been friendly with the Bennet ladies.

Fanny Bennet watched her daughter with a motherly eye. From this distance, she could not see Jane's expression, but she could read her posture. Shaking her head, Fanny bit back a sigh. She did not think Jane was enjoying the ball at all. Turning to Lady Derby, she said, "Sadly, they often seem more like flies." Careful to keep her face clear of concern, Mrs. Bennet's annoyance was only shown in her comment, "They hover annoyingly, and at times, bite."

Lady Derby turned back to Fanny and consoled, "Yes, you more than most understand that, and I can see why you worry about Jane. However, you know she is a strong girl and can hold her own. Some people may see her beauty and placid facade as weakness, but those that wish to take advantage will learn to regret it."

Laughing softly, Fanny said, "Sometimes I wonder how Lizzie would have handled a London season as a debutante. She certainly would not tolerate some of what I know Jane does for the sake of peace. Her need to see people treated well would have set her against the tabbies and the rakes in a trice."

Lady Derby was forced to hide her chuckle behind her fan. "I so love your Lizzie. I truly hope some of her vigor rubs off on my girls."

"I must thank you for encouraging her to take up archery. It has proven very helpful to Lizzie and the others." Fanny sometimes feared what would have happened if Lizzie hadn't taken to the sport. Not only did it seem to help Lizzie with her control and patience, but it had also already helped Kitty to build her own courage and self-confidence. That was even putting aside the time Kitty had to use her newfound skill for protection.

"It is no bother. My girls were too young to teach, and Lizzie was such a ball of energy at fourteen that I had to give her something to do. Now I have partners to practice and compete with." Lady Derby smiled as she spoke, but rather than watch the other people around the room, her attention remained on Mrs. Bennet.

Eventually Fanny realized where Lady Derby's attention lay, and quirking an eyebrow, asked, "Why do you look at me so? I know there is nothing wrong with my appearance."

"No, there is nothing wrong with your appearance. That is not what I was considering." Lady Derby's eyes narrowed slightly as she seemed to ponder something. "You know, I do not think anyone present would believe that you are thirty-nine. You could very well pass for a much younger woman. In fact, you are much prettier than half the debutantes of the season."

Fanny tilted her head, wondering what her friend was about. "While I will thank you for your compliment, I am wondering why you say such things."

"Have you considered remarrying?" Lady Derby fastened her eyes on Fanny, her face clear of artifice.

Shocked, Fanny reared back from Lady Derby, then, stepping closer, she hissed, "I am *still* married to a very unpleasant man. Why would you speak of me marrying another one?" Shaking her head slightly, Fanny looked back at the dancing people. Why would Lady Derby say such a thing? She really had no desire to trap herself again, even if she was still desirable.

"You know that Mr. Bennet will not live forever. In fact, with what I know of his dissolute lifestyle, I doubt he will live much longer. You could still have a chance at a loving marriage in the near future." Lady Derby's comment came as soft as a whisper but left Fanny feeling as though she had been struck by lightning.

She had tried to ignore any news she heard about her estranged husband, but she did know that after she and her girls had fled, he had gone bankrupt and was forced to find employment. Reports of him had become scarce since he arrived in London, but she knew her brother stayed up to date on his whereabouts and situation. Just thinking of the man, even safe in a ballroom free from his reach, sent shivers down her spine.

Glancing at Lady Derby, Fanny saw her concern. She knew that her friend's marriage had been a love match, and all evidence suggested that they still loved each other deeply, even after over a decade of marriage. Meanwhile, Fanny had fallen out of her infatuation with her husband Thomas after two days of wedded bliss. "I know you only want to see me as happy in marriage as you are, but please do not try to get me to dream of something that, at least for now, cannot be. If I become a widow, I promise to think about what you have said. Until then, however, let us discuss more pleasant things."

Nodding in agreement, Lady Derby smiled and said, "All right, my dear. I hear you went to the opera last week. What did you think of the new stage set? I hear it is quite beautiful."

FINDING HER MOTHER AND Lady Derby talking happily in a little alcove, Jane quietly joined them. Her next dance partner had yet to claim her for their set, so she had a moment to relax without worry. Without interrupting their conversation, Jane studied the two women. Of similar ages, they were both beautiful, though Jane found that her mother's blue eyes seemed to have a more serious look about them.

Her mother was still remarkably attractive for all that she had two daughters over twenty. It helped that she was seventeen when she had Jane. It was easy to see that Jane had inherited her looks from her mother—both women blonde and blue-eyed. Some people might say that it was a gift to have inherited her looks, but Jane knew her mother's beauty had not done her any favors.

Jane was unsure that her own beauty would benefit her any more than her mother's had. Her mother's appearance had won her the attention of the heir to Longbourn, who turned out was not worthy of the title gentleman. Then Fanny had been stuck at Longbourn for over two decades, dealing with his cruelty and negligence before Lizzie and Mr. Darcy had found a way to force his hand.

The Bennet ladies had finally escaped his dominion, but Jane wondered if anyone but her sister Elizabeth was truly liberated. Though they all fought his influence with every step they took, they were all still haunted by their past.

Mrs. Bennet's cobalt eyes scanned Jane before she said, "You look as if you have had enough this evening. Would you like to go home, sweetheart?"

Shaking her head, Jane sighed and said, "No, I do not want to be rude. I still have several more sets claimed, though I started turning gentlemen down before my card was full."

Snapping her fan shut, Lady Derby contradicted her. "Don't be silly. I shall say that your mother has been affected by a megrim and you, being the dutiful daughter that you are, accompanied her home to care for her. They will only laud you for your sweet disposition even more. You are the season's diamond, after all."

Rubbing at the center of her forehead where an ache was forming, Jane groaned. "Don't remind me."

Coming to her side, Lady Derby gave her hand a squeeze. "You poor dear, these fools cannot see your true worth, and they are idiots for it."

Looking at the older woman, Jane smiled in gratitude. Few people knew that Lady Derby was her Aunt Gardiner's cousin. Both women were compassionate and intelligent in equal measures, and there was much about them that Jane wanted to emulate. She was not as close to Lady Derby as Elizabeth or Kitty were, but she had been sponsoring her for her bow before the queen and throughout all the ensuing activities.

Jane hugged Lady Derby, saying quietly, "You are a dear. I do not think I could keep my equanimity if my next partner was at all like my last one."

Narrowing her eyes at the comment, Lady Derby asked, "Ungentlemanly or idiotic? I can do much about the first, but little about the second."

Fighting to keep her face calm, Jane replied, "No, not ungentlemanly, merely idiotic, but I shall not worry my pretty little head about it, for I have escaped him. Thank you for helping me to escape the evening."

"It is what I am here for, my dear." Turning to Jane's mother, she said, "It was lovely to chat with you again, Fanny. We really should get together for tea soon."

"Of course. I will send you a note tomorrow." Kissing her friend's cheek, Fanny linked arms with Jane before walking towards the exit.

ONCE IN THE CARRIAGE, Jane relaxed into the squabs. Watching listlessly out the window into the darkness. She would be glad to get back to the Gardiners' home, where she could change into something more comfortable and try to fall asleep.

"You look done in, my dear. Are you keeping too busy a schedule?" Her mother's voice came to her through the darkness of the rocking carriage.

"Perhaps, Mama. I have been busier before, but so many of these gatherings are superficial and without meaning and it saps me of all my joy." Smoothing her hands down the texture of her dress in a soothing fashion, Jane sighed. "I just want to go home."

"We should be at my brother's soon," her mother responded gently.

Jane wished she could be soothed by the reassurance in her mother's voice. It was simply no longer possible. Not after a month of being hounded and treated to the superficiality of the ton. It seemed as if every day had twisted her into tighter knots. If she did not put an end to it soon, she felt as if she would snap like a too taut bowstring. "No, Mama. As much as I love Aunt and Uncle Gardiner, I do not wish to be here in London anymore. I miss my still room. I miss working in the garden, and I miss helping people who need it."

Jane heard a sharp intake of breath come from the other side of the carriage before her mother said, "Oh Janie, I know. As hard as it was at Longbourn, there are things about it that I miss too, but you know we cannot go back." Jane could hear the anxiety in her mother's voice at the mere mention of Longbourn and hated herself for the pain she had brought her.

As carefully as she could in a dark, rocking carriage, Jane moved to sit next to her mother to soothe her as best she could. Looping her arm through her mother's, she snuggled into Fanny's side. "I do not mean Longbourn, Mama. I do not mean that garden or still room. What I meant is that I yearn for the satisfaction of accomplishing those tasks. This way of life is not the way I wish to live." Happy to feel the tension leave her mother, Jane added, "I do not want to bother Lizzie and her new husband, but we have been away from Pemberley for a month. Do you think that they would mind if we returned early?"

"I know we were trying to give the newlyweds some time to themselves, but I cannot imagine your sister being anything but thrilled to see you." Patting her daughter's knee, she continued, "If you are sure that this is what you want, we can begin making arrangements tomorrow."

"Yes, Mama, I am more than sure." Jane felt stress bleed out of her at the mere thought of being able to flee London. She began thinking of what must be done in order to leave, as well as what she might do once they arrived at Pemberley.

She continued, "Despite Aunt Gardiner's assurances that she is fine with the four of us staying with her for the season, I know it has but a strain on the household to accommodate us. I am sure we can find ways to be helpful at Pemberley."

"I fear you might be correct." Repositioning herself, Fanny said, "Maybe Mr. Darcy would consider allowing us to take up residence in the dower house."

Jane laughed softly into the cool air of the night. "You know, he told you he wanted you to call him son, and if not, then William would do. He also did not want to hear of us trying to hide away in one of the cottages or the dower house. I was there when he pointed out that there are more than enough rooms in the family wing to house us all with more to spare."

"Your sister has certainly landed herself a generous man. I do believe he is one of the good ones, Jane," said Fanny.

"Yes, he is." Jane thought of what a wonderful match Elizabeth and Darcy had made. Sometimes in the middle of the night, when Jane could not sleep, she would think about all that had occurred to bring them together and how much they had to overcome. Their love had been the tipping point that enabled the Bennet ladies to leave Longbourn.

Thinking of Elizabeth and Mr. Darcy caused Jane's mind to wander to Mr. Bingley. It had been easier at the beginning of her season when he had also been in London, and she could depend on at least one gentleman at the events she attended. When he had left London to see his sister and new little nephew back in Netherfield, it had become more difficult for her.

Biting back an uneasy sigh so as to not worry her mother, Jane contemplated her relationship with Mr. Bingley. They had met at an assembly back in Meryton and Jane had quickly found him just what a man should be. He was handsome, and while Elizabeth had always leaned towards tall, dark, and handsome, Jane's inclination had often taken another path. In fact, Mr. Bingley's fair coloring, with striking blue eyes and wavy copper locks, suited her quite well.

Because Jane was always ready to look beneath the surface, she saw more than just his superficial appearance. He was amiable, and though he had obvious holes in his knowledge of what it was to be a landholder, he was inclined to learn to fill those gaps. When called for, he had proven himself capable in a crisis and was willing to stand up for what was right. Of least concern was his financial standing. Though Jane was aware of how crucial it was to be able to support a wife and children, Jane did not require the fine dresses and jewels that other women might find vital.

Mr. Bingley seemed to have all the qualities she wanted in a man, yet she hesitated. Jane was well aware of the fact that her mother had thought herself in love when she had married her father. Not only had it proven to be a hollow infatuation, but she had suffered for decades for her lack of insight. Jane was terrified of making such a mistake.

Jane had been grappling with her emotions, fully aware of the gravity of the decision she faced regarding marriage. As much as she wanted to marry a man she loved, she did not want emotion to lead her down an unsavory path. It was not until Mr. Bingley had left to see his sister and he had been less present in her life that she realized how much her feelings were already engaged. She missed him, his laugh, and the way he always had an encouraging smile ready, no matter the situation.

Mr. Bingley had kindly let her know that though he had feelings for her, he wanted her to have a season and not feel obligated to reciprocate. He knew she had been confined by her situation back at Longbourn and had never had the chance to even consider marriage before she met him. Her father's cruel desire to keep his family trapped in misery had stifled her thoughts of marriage. Adjusting to a world of new possibilities was proving more difficult than she had hoped. Mr. Bingley knew this and wanted to give her the chance to choose the man she wanted to be with, even if that was not him. He had encouraged her to widen her circle, have a season, and even explore who she was away from Longbourn and her father.

Jane was conflicted. She felt as though she could love Mr. Bingley, if only for his unselfish desire to help her see more of the world. Still, she worried if he saw the real Jane. More than once, she had heard him comment on how beautiful she was. Mr. Bingley was also rather fond of the word *angel*. Both statements had left her unsettled, though Jane had never said as much to Mr. Bingley. She knew that he was trying to compliment her, and she would never be so churlish as to complain, though it left her wondering, did he see more than her superficial beauty?

She was more than just her blonde hair and deep blue eyes. If he saw her true worth, then he might make the perfect husband. The question was, did he see everything that was *her* when he looked at her, or was he only seeing what was on the outside? She supposed she needed to find a way to puzzle it out.

If he was actually seeing the real Jane, shouldn't she let herself go enough to truly fall in love? Was it something she was even capable of?

Chapter Two

Bingley attempted to keep his head resting securely against the back of the cushions of his carriage, only to be flung forward once again. Recent weather had damaged the roads and even with a carriage as well sprung as his, the ride was proving to be uncomfortable. It would be less of a hardship if he had not been so tired and out of sorts. On the road to Pemberley from Netherfield, Bingley had too much time to let his mind wander.

His time at Netherfield with his family had been both amazing and painful. His sister Louisa had come through her ordeal splendidly, according to Aunt Guthrie. Though seeing her afterward, wan and exhausted, he personally wondered what she would have looked like if she had come through poorly. He knew that childbirth was dangerous to both mother and child, so seeing them both well was a relief.

Her husband, Hurst, doted on his wife, doing everything he could to ensure that she was well and recovering from their son's birth. It seemed that their once less than stellar relationship had grown into something more, and Bingley was happy for his sister and the love that she now had in her marriage. Watching them gaze down at their child so tenderly brought a bittersweet ache to his heart.

Bingley's brother-in-law was so very proud of his son. They had named him Felton. Felton? It was not a name that Bingley would have chosen for his nephew, but apparently it was a Hurst family tradition to name the first-born son and heir to the estate Felton. He already had plans to teach the boy a strong right hook before he went off to school. It was the least he could do as a proud uncle.

Life with an infant was a new experience for him, but that did not mean that he wasn't ready to try to help. He had taken many a turn with the crying babe, who was uncertain of the new world that he had been presented with. Snuggling the small lad to his chest, Bingley would walk with him about the house, trying to get him to sleep. Only caring for Felton had left him longing for things that he was uncertain he would be able to have. Bingley found himself realizing just how much he wanted a child of his own—boy or girl, it did not matter—and more than anything, he wanted that child to be Jane Bennet's.

Eventually, his Aunt Guthrie took him aside. "Charles, enough of this gloomy attitude. Why are you moping about when there is so much to celebrate?"

It had been a surprise that he had been so easily read. He had thought he had been doing a tolerable job of hiding his odd sort of envy. Bingley found himself rubbing at the back of his neck in an anxious fashion and saying, "I had hoped I was not so transparent."

Reaching out, Aunt Guthrie brushed a lock of his hair back from his forehead in a motherly fashion. Her voice was soft as she said, "To someone who knows you as well as I do, you are quite transparent. I suspect I know why being around a beautiful new family is so painful for you, but I want to hear your explanation."

Bingley knew there was no avoiding his aunt's question, and there was a strong possibility that she would have some parental words of wisdom that he could benefit from. He could feel his shoulders drooping as he confessed, "Though I do not begrudge my sister's happiness with her new child, it has brought home just how much I want such things for myself."

Looking at her nephew with raised eyebrows, she said, "I have a feeling that it is not just a wife and child that you want. It is a *particular* wife whose child you want." Bingley knew that his aunt had been very fond of Miss Bennet when they had met the previous autumn. Somehow, he was not surprised that his aunt was able to decipher where his thoughts lay. "I hear Miss Bennet is in London this season and has become quite the diamond. You know that you could return to her there. Your sister and nephew are not in such desperate need of help that you have to stay."

Shaking his head, he said, "I do not think I could stand another ball where I am forced to witness yet more gentlemen traipse after her."

"You are trying to be noble by allowing her a choice. I can appreciate that, but I am quite confident that your Miss Bennet will not fall for any of the practiced pleasantries found in London ballrooms. She has more sense than that." Tilting her head, Guthrie locked eyes with Bingley before continuing, "I have things well in hand, and your sister and Hurst will need to learn how to manage on their own soon enough. Staying here will only put you further out of sorts. I do believe that it is time for you to go. You do not need to go to London, but you should not stay here."

One did not argue with Bingley's Aunt Guthrie if they had any sense. Netherfield may have technically been his leased property, but she was not the matriarch of his family for nothing. So Bingley had packed up and set off on his way to Pemberley.

Recent marriage aside, surely his friend would welcome a visit. Bingley would make himself useful somehow and keep his eye out for any nearby estates for sale. If he won Miss Bennet's heart, he wanted to settle near her sister. Miss Bennet and Mrs. Darcy were exceedingly close, and he would hate to be the reason to separate them to an unbearable extent.

Thinking of how close the Bennet sisters were made him think of his own siblings, for all he was riding away from them. He had grown much closer to both of his sisters on this last visit. Surprisingly, even his time with Caroline had been a pleasure. It seemed that her time in Scotland with Aunt Guthrie had been just what she needed. It was almost as if he had his old sister back, the one he had known before his parents had sent her to that finishing school. He only hoped that the changes would stick.

Sighing, Bingley closed his eyes, wondering if it was possible for him to fall asleep while moving over the rutted road. While he had been up some nights offering to walk the poor fretful babe when he had colic, Bingley had not been sleeping well for quite some time before that. Bingley's nights had been haunted by bad dreams. In one particularly unsettling dream, he saw Miss Bennet adorned with a shimmering crown, setting sail with a foreign prince, while leaving him alone and forsaken on the docks.

Rubbing at his forehead, Bingley considered the journey from Hertfordshire to Derbyshire. He knew it would take several days to reach Pemberley, depending on the weather and the condition of the roads. It occurred to him that he had not sent an express to tell his friend of his upcoming arrival, but that was no great issue; he would simply write a letter at whatever inn he stopped at. It would be good to see Darcy, even if watching his happiness with his wife was almost painful. He wanted that kind of love with Miss Bennet. Maybe he could ask for some advice from one or both of them.

For now, his greatest hope was that none of the gentlemen in London would claim Miss Bennet's heart before he could prove himself to her. He fell asleep thinking of his angel and the kind of life he wanted to live with her.

GLANCING OUT THE WINDOW, Elizabeth asked, "Is that a carriage?"

Looking up from his ledger, Darcy craned his neck to get a glimpse. Eyebrows drawing together in confusion, Darcy put his papers down and walked to the window. There appeared to be a carriage on the drive. Turning to Elizabeth, who was sitting by the window using the light to work on a little gown for one of the expectant tenant mothers, he said, "I thought your family would be arriving tomorrow?"

"I thought so too." Putting her work down and carefully tucking it away into her sewing basket, she stood. "Perhaps something about their plans changed? I will speak with Mrs. Reynolds about refreshments and fresh water in their rooms." Walking toward the doorway, she was stopped when Darcy called out to her.

"My dear, you could simply ring for her. You do not have to go searching her out. Pemberley is a much bigger place to search through than Longbourn."

Screwing up her face, Elizabeth shrugged her shoulders and went to the bellpull. The task completed, she walked to Darcy and leaned into his side, looking out the window with him. "I know that very well." Reaching up on her tiptoes, she kissed his cheek, her eyes dancing at the fire that flared in his eyes. "It is a good thing I was such an excellent walker before I arrived here, Wills, otherwise you might find me taking up residence on one of the many landings of the many staircases."

Darcy might have responded to Elizabeth's teasing manner with the more substantial kiss he wanted if it weren't for the throat clearing at the doorway. Closing his eyes for a moment, Darcy blew out a breath. More than one staff member had come upon him kissing Elizabeth; at least this time he had not yet done so. It did not, however, help his frustration. Looking at the maid, whose cheeks had developed a slight blush, Darcy tried to focus back on the matter at hand. There had been a reason for which they had summoned the girl...wasn't there?

Elizabeth did not move an inch. Still leaning into him, she addressed the staff while Darcy was still trying to remove his attention from her lips. "Joan, there is a carriage approaching. I think it might be my family coming from London. I would like to make sure refreshments are provided in half an hour. The family rooms they will be staying in have already been prepared, but I would like to make sure there is fresh water for them to use." Pausing, Elizabeth tilted her head before continuing, "That is, of course, if it is my mother and sisters. It could very well be someone else, but I would like to see to their comfort either way."

It reassured Darcy when Mrs. Reynolds had said the staff, for the most part, were happy to see that the master and mistress were indeed thrilled in their new marriage. Apparently, it boded well for the future of Pemberley. Darcy had never considered how the staff might feel working under an unhappy couple. It would certainly not help the servants if the lord and lady of the house existed in stony silence or, worse yet, heated arguments.

Once they were alone again, Darcy looked down into Elizabeth's shining expression and asked, "Shall we head out to greet them, my love?"

Elizabeth grinned infectiously and said, "Yes, let's."

Swooping down, Darcy allowed himself one brief kiss before offering her his arm and escorting her to the front steps where they could greet their guests. As they stood at the top of the steps waiting for the carriage to finish its journey, Elizabeth turned to look at him, a hint of concern in her expression. "What has you worried, Lizziebet?"

Pursing her lips, she furrowed her brow as she asked, "I know my family had intended to stay in London much longer. You are not upset that they are coming back early, are you? I would never want you to be disappointed or concerned that I do not devote enough attention to you." Reaching up, Elizabeth smoothed his waistcoat and straightened his cravat, which had become slightly askew.

Catching her hands, he held them to his chest over his heart. "I may not love your mother and sisters as much as you do, but I am more than simply fond of them. They are my mother and sisters, and I am glad to see to their wellbeing and happiness. If they are not suited to London, I cannot find fault in it. I am not overly fond of the city myself." Pulling her right hand to his mouth, he kissed her palm. "Were you upset when Georgianna did not want to go with them to London and chose to stay at Pemberley with us?"

Shaking her head, Elizabeth was quick to reassure Darcy. "No, of course not. Georgie is lovely company, and I enjoy spending time with her when you are busy with estate business."

Smiling, Darcy kissed her palm again, this time letting his lips linger before saying, "Exactly. Besides, Pemberley is expansive, and you yourself said that our suite is so large that we could live in it and not come out for a month if we wanted to. If I feel neglected, I shall just steal you away and keep you all to myself." Darcy had been so lost in Elizabeth's emerald eyes that he had not realized the carriage had arrived until he heard the laughter.

Startled, Darcy turned to his friend. "Bingley! I had no notion you were to visit us." Wrapping his arm around Elizabeth's waist as Bingley jogged up the steps, he said, "We saw the carriage and came out to greet our visitors but did not expect to see you."

Bingley shook his head, his eyes twinkling as he laughed. "Yes, and while you waited, you became distracted. You know, Darcy, now that you are married, you can leave off all of that romance foolishness. You already have her; it is not as though she can get away."

Narrowing her eyes, Elizabeth glared at their visitor, though her lips twitching gave her humor away as she said, "If you try to convince my husband to stop with the romance, I will start using you for target practice. I have been trying to come up with a way to practice on a moving object and you just might do."

Darcy looked over at his friend and noticed the fatigue etched on his face. Bingley's eyes seemed to be bruised and puffy, and though he laughed and smiled with them, his normal effervescence was lacking. "Bingley, how is your sister? Your last letter, though ink stained and hard to read, was full of the happy news of a baby boy. I thought you would stay with her for some time."

"Louisa is well and recovering nicely, according to Aunt Guthrie. She said it was time for me to leave. Apparently, the young couple will have to learn to cope without my assistance. Rubbing his hand down his face Bingley continued, "As much as I love little Felton, I will admit that it feels as if I have not slept well for what seems like weeks."

Nodding at his news, Elizabeth gestured Bingley into the house. "Well, you are always welcome at Pemberley. Let us get you inside. I have asked for refreshments to be made ready. We can sit and chat while I have your guest room made up."

Bingley let his body relax into the offered chair with a sigh. He felt every rock and rut that his carriage ran over on the three-day journey to Pemberley. He was more than looking forward to the comfort of his bed this evening.

"I am surprised you did not send word that you were coming." Bingley could read the concern on his old friend's face when Darcy spoke.

"I was going to write to you at the first inn I stopped at but was so tired I completely forgot." Rubbing his gritty eyes, Bingley sat up straighter in his chair and searched the pockets of his rumpled attire. Groaning, he produced a letter and sheepishly handed it to Darcy. "The second night I wrote a note, but it appears I forgot to send it off to you."

Darcy accepted the note with a chuckle. "You always did poorly when you did not get enough sleep. I can remember that time you stayed up late studying for Professor Jinkins's test and you were so inattentive that you tried to throw your test sheet away instead of turning it in."

"I remember that. It is a good thing that old Jinkins liked me and fetched it out of the rubish." Bingley laughed at the memory. "I actually got top marks, but Jinkins advised me to get more sleep before my next test because another professor might not be as generous."

He and Darcy were still laughing over some of their school experiences when Mrs. Darcy came into the room shortly before the tea service arrived. Standing next to the teapot, she asked, "Mr. Bingley, you look like you could do with a restorative cup of tea, if you do not mind my saying so."

Bingley turned his gaze to her and smiled gratefully. "I would love a cup, Mrs. Darcy. Thank you." While she readied his tea, Bingley studied Mrs. Darcy. Most people did not see any familial resemblance between Miss Bennet and Mrs. Darcy, but he could see it clearly.

The two oldest Bennet daughters may have been night and day, dark brown hair versus shining blonde, emerald eyes instead of sapphire ones, but he saw where they were the same. They had the same arch in their brows and their noses had the same pert tip. Their beauty aside, it was what lay beneath that truly made the sisters alike. While some did not see it because Miss Bennet always wore her smile like armor, both sisters were unending kindness wrapped around a core of steel.

Accepting his cup of tea, Bingley took an eager sip, nearly scalding his tongue. It was just this side of too hot. He looked up from his cup of tea just in time to watch Darcy and his wife have a silent conversation with their eyes. It ended with her raised eyebrows and a tilt of her head, while Darcy was grinning wide enough to show off his dimples.

Turning to Bingley, Mrs. Darcy said, "I will leave you two gentlemen to reminisce. I think your usual room should be ready soon, but I will go check on things while you talk." She left the room, but not without glancing over her shoulder at her husband with a grin.

Darcy watched her go before turning back to Bingley and asking, "So why were you studying *my* Elizabeth so closely?" Stretching out his legs, he crossed them at the ankles before continuing, "I know you do not have designs on my wife, but I am still curious."

Feeling his cheeks heat in a slight blush, Bingley muttered, "You saw that, did you?"

"Yes."

Sighing, Bingley took another sip of his tea to fortify himself for the conversation he thought was at hand. "Your wife looks very much like her sister."

Nodding at the explanation, Darcy took a sip of his own teacup but said nothing. Bingley knew his friend's behavior was designed to get him to confess all. It was, in fact, a practice he had seen his own father use. You let the silence continue until your opponent felt the need to cover the silence with their words. He knew Darcy did not see him as an opponent, but it seemed that Darcy, or possibly Mrs. Darcy, wanted to get something out of him.

Well, it was not like he was trying to hide anything. Not really, anyway. "The way she raised her eyebrows just a bit, Miss Bennet does the same when she is concerned about someone. In that moment, I realized I could see a lot of Miss Bennet's traits in her younger sister."

Looking at his friend in a discerning way, Darcy said, "I am surprised that you would want to come here and not go to London for the season."

Shaking his head, Bingley said, "I could not watch her being followed by all the sycophants anymore. I know I encouraged her to spread her wings and enjoy the season, and I want that for her, I do, but it was eating me up." Putting his teacup down on a side table, Bingley began to pace, running his hands through his hair as he did so. "None of them see her for what she is. They only chase after her for her beauty, and it is not fair to her."

"Do you see her for what she is?" Darcy did not move from his chair, but watched his friend sympathetically as he moved around the room.

"How could I not? You know, I think I have spent more time with her than any woman besides my family." Stopping to gaze at the fire, Bingley attempted to assemble his thoughts into a more cogent pattern. "I have seen her stand up for what was important to her. How she stood up to Caroline was magnificent. While she is almost always kind, she never allows that kindness to prevent her from doing what must be done. It does not make her weak either. Though I have seen people in London try to take advantage of her, she has always stood firm."

"It seems as if you know her. Does she know that?" Darcy questioned, his head tilted and eyebrows drawn.

"I am uncertain. You know how all the Bennet ladies suffered at Longbourn. I have not wanted to pressure her into anything that would cause her discomfort." Sitting back down, Bingley leaned forward in his chair, facing Darcy with enthusiasm. "But despite trying not to pressure her, I have had the time to study her, to learn about her. I have come to know how truly beautiful she is."

"I do not think there is a man in England who would disagree with you." Darcy took a sip of his tea before adding, "Though you will forgive me if I prefer my wife's looks to that of her sister."

"We never had similar tastes when it came to women." Bingley rubbed at the back of his neck, smiling ruefully. "While I agree that any man in the world and see her beauty, it is not what I mean when I say that."

Stopping to take his teacup back up, Bingley took a sip. Then, looking at Darcy, he wondered if he was trying to play the devil's advocate. Bingley knew Darcy had become very protective of all the Bennet ladies, even Mrs. Bennet. It was possible that Darcy was testing him, getting him to prove his worth to them both.

"Jane's beauty is in how she loves, the way that she protects those that need it, and her willingness to sacrifice for the good of others. It makes me want to protect her and make sure that there is at least one person who is looking out for her when she is not always looking out for herself." Bingley's words felt as if they had been drawn from his very being, as if he had never said anything so true before that moment.

"Then I approve." Darcy tipped his teacup to Bingley in a salute.

Rolling his eyes, Bingley accepted the approval. Not that he ever truly thought his friend would disapprove of the match. "Thank you, but I do not see what good that does me. She is in London being courted by other men, and I am here."

Darcy's brown eyes seemed to hold a mischievous gleam that was quite rare to see. Quirking his lips in a half smile, he said, "And that is where you would be wrong."

Bingley's grip tightened on his teacup before he carefully put it down with numb fingers. Could his friend be implying what he thought he was implying? "Pardon?"

Smiling rather smugly, Darcy replied, "My sister by marriage is currently on the road from London with the rest of her sisters and mother. They should arrive sometime tomorrow." He waited a moment, and Bingley found himself swallowing convulsively before Darcy added, "In fact, we thought it was them coming up the drive when you showed up just now."

"I cannot believe the coincidence." Jumping back up to pace some more, Bingley's mind started filtering through too many questions and hopes to process. "Do you know why they are returning early? Are they well? Do you think I have a chance at winning her heart? Do you know of any estates up for sale nearby in case I do?"

Standing up, Darcy went to his friend and clasped him on the shoulder, waiting for him to run out of steam before saying, "As far as

I know, they are all well, but as for why they left London, I think you will have to ask *Jane* yourself. You have a better chance of winning her than anyone else I know, and I know of one or two estates that might suit, but you should probably wait until you are further along in the relationship before purchasing anything." Darcy started guiding his friend towards the hall. "Your room should be ready by now. You can wash and rest before we dine tonight. Get a good night's sleep. It will probably be better if you do not look exhausted when you see her tomorrow."

Chapter Three

Looking out the window of the carriage, Jane was grateful to recognize the landmarks that meant they were near Pemberley. She was uncertain if she would have been able to manage another day of travel. She had developed a headache the morning before, and no matter what she did to combat the pain, it had lingered and only worsened.

Even the quiet chatter between Kitty and Lydia was sending shards of pain through her skull. Settling back into the cushions of the carriage, Jane forced a smile onto her face. That morning, she had been able to pretend to sleep and block out the light, but it would not do at the moment, not when they were so close to their destination. Maybe the headache would recede when they finally stopped rocking back and forth.

To take her mind off her suffering, Jane tried to list the things that she wanted to do now that she had finally escaped the city. She wanted to check in on the herb garden. It had only been a month or so since she had explored the garden last, but there was such a difference in the garden once spring was evident. Now, with spring spreading its eager tendrils, she was sure she could get a better picture of what she had to work with. An estate's still room depended so much on what they were able to grow and what was available to purchase. For that reason, it was important for all that the garden was well maintained.

Elizabeth had said there was already so much for her to get used to in being the mistress of such an expansive estate and was more than happy to let Jane help oversee the garden and still room. It made sense. Jane enjoyed the task so much and she had the most experience, for that matter.

Then there was the still room itself. Jane would need to inventory the supplies and find out if Pemberley produced its own soaps and lotions, or whether they purchased them. She would also need to stock up on tinctures for spring colds. With all her planning, Jane managed to keep her mind distracted until they finally came to a stop at the steps of Pemberley. Still, her distraction meant that the moment her mind returned to the situation at hand, she became even more aware of her affliction.

Waiting at the bottom of the steps with her husband gave Elizabeth the strange sense of déjà vu. Had it only been the day before that they had welcomed Bingley? At least this time, they hadn't been caught *distracted*. Rushing forward to hug her mother as she descended the steps of the carriage, Elizabeth rejoiced at having her family back home with her. She knew that most new brides would expect to be separated from their families, but Elizabeth could not help but be glad that was not the case for her, at least not yet.

Like metal in a fiery forge, the bond between her and her mother and sisters had been tested and strengthened during their time at Longbourn. They were closer than typical families, having depended upon each other for everything for so long. She loved William, but as much as she loved him, it felt as though part of her was missing when her mother and sisters had left.

Now it was as if all the missing pieces of her heart had been found, and she felt complete. Gazing around the circle, she took them all in—Kitty and Lydia were chatting, and though Kitty seemed the same, it looked as though Lydia had once again grown. Lydia would soon be the tallest of them all. Mary was much the same as the last she had seen her. The only change she noticed was that Mary was wearing a new dress that Elizabeth thought was very flattering for traveling attire.

Elizabeth had worried that things had gone badly in London when her mother had written about their desire to leave the metropolis. Her fears were confirmed when she spotted Jane coming out of the carriage. Jane had changed in a way that did not sit well with Elizabeth at all. Though Jane's smile remained, little lines around her eyes and the brittleness of her expression spoke of pain, both emotional and physical. Going to Jane, she wrapped her in a hug and then linked arms with her, escorting her into the house.

"I am sure you all would love a chance to refresh yourselves, or we could have tea first, if you prefer. Your rooms are ready for you should you want to rest before dinner." Stopping in the hall near the grand staircase, Elizabeth offered them the opportunity to choose their course of action.

Looking at her older sisters, Lydia was the first to speak. "I do not know about everyone else, but I am so thirsty I could drink a muddy puddle."

"Really, Lydia, you are beyond the bounds of all expectation," Mary sighed. Though her words might have implied disfavor, her tone easily showed her love and acceptance of her younger sister's occasional boisterous ways.

Laughing unabashedly, Elizabeth went to Lydia and, hugging her tightly, said, "I have missed you so. No one behaves quite as unexpectedly as you." Leaning back slightly, Elizabeth looked at her sister with raised brows. "I take it to mean that you would like to have tea?"

Smiling merrily, Lydia replied, "Yes, please."

By seemingly mutual agreement, they all headed into the sitting room for some tea and refreshments while their trunks were brought up to their rooms. "Surprisingly, we have a guest who arrived yesterday. I did not have any time to let you know, but I hope his arrival will be looked upon with excitement."

JANE IMMEDIATELY SAW THE person subtly mentioned by her sister. Standing by the unlit fireplace was the man that she had been contemplating of late. Even from across the room, she could see him stand straighter, perking up at her entrance to the room.

For a moment, Jane was frozen, the lingering pain in her head making it too hard to determine her next actions. Should she go over and greet him as she wished, or should she allow him to make his way over to her? Simply seeing him had forced her to realize how much she had missed him. Despite the pain she was fighting, it was as if seeing him had made everything lighter.

In the end, her hesitation had taken the choice out of her hands because he was approaching her. As he approached Jane, he appeared as though he had almost wanted to reach out to her, but stopped himself, letting his hand drop back down to his side. "Miss Bennet, I am pleased to see you again." Smiling faintly, he stepped even closer and lowered his voice. "Please tell me how I may be of assistance?"

The instinctual drawing together of her brows sent pain stabbing through her head. Closing her eyes for a moment, she breathed through the pain before opening them as he took her softly by the arm, escorting her over to one of the comfortable chairs in the corner of the room. Sitting down with a sigh, she looked up at him in confusion.

Bingley kneeled next to her chair and said, "I can see that you are in pain. What can I do to help you?"

Jane vaguely registered Georgianna joining the party and chatting with Kitty and Lydia in the opposite corner while Elizabeth was speaking discreetly with a maid, but her focus remained on the man kneeling before her. Her eyes widened. How had he known? She had figured that both her mother and Elizabeth were aware of her issue. Jane knew they were only holding back out of respect, but would most likely say something soon. However, Mr. Bingley's knowledge of the situation puzzled her.

Swallowing, she looked into his concerned eyes and replied, "It is merely a megrim. I will manage."

Keeping his voice gentle, he continued, "But surely there is something that can be done to alleviate your pain."

Jane watched a little notch appear between Mr. Bingley's furrowed brows in fascination, feeling oddly disconnected from the moment. "Sometimes a dark room or a cool compress helps, but I do not wish to be rude. I will retire to my room and ask for some willow bark tea once everyone is finished socializing." Jane knew her sister would want to socialize with everyone. If she asked to go directly to her room, Elizabeth and her sisters would worry. She could manage a little longer.

Jane watched Mr. Bingley struggle for a moment, almost as if he wanted to contest her statement. Looking around the room, he watched everyone chatting for a moment before turning back to her. "And what would you do if you knew that it was Miss Kitty who was the one suffering from a megrim?"

Shaking her head slightly, Jane realized what he was about before muttering, "Nothing different—I would put her to bed in a dark room with a cool compress and willow bark tea."

Seeming to fight a grin, he contested her logic. "But I am sure you would not wait to finish socializing before you put her to bed. You would see to it immediately."

Elizabeth approached the softly talking couple and interjected, "You are completely correct, Mr. Bingley. My sister would never let one of us suffer in order to enjoy herself." Elizabeth smiled faintly at Mr. Bingley before turning her attention back to Jane. "I have asked a maid to close the curtains in your room. She is getting you willow bark tea and a cool compress. Your lady's maid will help make you more comfortable. I will have a tray sent up to you later in case you feel you can stomach something. I want you to rest above stairs until at least tomorrow."

As Jane observed the strength of her younger sister's gaze, she was persuaded to acquiesce. Jane glanced across the room and saw her mother speaking with William while making a shooing motion toward her. It appeared that everyone agreed that it was time for her to go lay down, and frankly, the idea sounded lovely. Knowing that her smile must look closer to a wince, Jane softly thanked her sister.

"Your family will all still be here to spend time with once you are well," said Mr. Bingley. Offering his arm, he helped her to stand and escorted her to the stairs.

Quietly thanking him for his assistance, Jane began ascending the stairs with Elizabeth's arm linked through her own. Fighting her pain, Jane tried to sort through what had just happened. It still confused her that Mr. Bingley had not only seen her pain but had tried to encourage her to see to herself, just as her mother or Elizabeth might do.

They had made it mostly to her room in silence before Elizabeth said, "You know your headache will not improve if you continue thinking that hard."

"I do not know if it is the megrim or something else, but I cannot understand—how did he know I was in pain?" Reaching the room she stayed in when at Pemberley, Elizabeth escorted Jane inside. The darkness of the room almost instantly helped to relieve some of her suffering.

Elizabeth spoke softly, but not without humor. "How indeed?" Kissing Jane's cheek, she continued, "Let Dawson help you and try to turn off the questions running around in your head. Drink your tea and go to sleep. I will see you in the morning."

JANE DREW THE COOL morning air into her lungs. She stood at her open window, looking out over the gardens. With the sun not yet fully risen, everything was painted in violet and mauve tones. Fog crept delicately over the grounds, wandering through the maze of the subtly hued scene. The sight was rather soothing. Letting the tranquility soak into her, Jane sighed in relief.

The pain that had been excruciating only yesterday had receded to a mere whisper, something Jane was certain she could cope with easily. It was even possible that she could banish it entirely with a cup of coffee and breakfast with her family.

Stepping back from the window, Jane moved to the comfortable chair near her fireplace. It would be some time before anyone besides possibly Elizabeth and William were up, and Jane was determined to use the peace and quiet for reflection. Taking up her paisley shawl, Jane settled it around her shoulders and curled up in her most comfortable chair.

While she did not have the brilliant mind that Elizabeth possessed, she was not incapable of thinking logically. She simply did not enjoy turning her thoughts towards the kinds of complicated topics her sister took pleasure in. Before she went down to face the morning, Jane was determined to have settled her mind and her anxious worries.

First of all, she did not enjoy her London season. The fact that she had left it well before the halfway point was certainly enough proof of that. While Jane might enjoy a few things the town offered, the marriage mart was not on that list. This did not mean, however, that she did not want to marry. Now that Jane was free from worrying about her father, she wished for a husband and children of her own very much. This acknowledgement swiftly turned her mind in the direction of Mr. Bingley. She would admit that she liked him. It was even possible that she more than liked him. But was that emotion enough to build a relationship on?

Jane twirled a strand of her blonde hair around her finger absentmindedly while she considered the concept. She knew that

Mr. Bingley also had feelings for her, but Jane wanted more assurance than mere feelings. She had witnessed where *feelings* had led her mother and though she did not discount them, she needed more than feelings to base on such an important decision. It was not that she did not trust Mr. Bingley per se; it was the fact that marriage would so thoroughly put her under his control. She had only recently gained some control in her life, and it was frightening to think that she could lose it so completely.

Beyond feelings, what did she desire? What would reassure her? Bringing her knees up to her chest, Jane rested her chin on her knees and closed her eyes, searching her heart. She wanted to know that she was truly seen. One of the reasons she had not enjoyed her recent time in London was she had not felt seen by anyone. Her beauty and her constant smile were all that people saw, but she was more than that. The mask was, at times, a reflex, especially when she was uneasy. It was an instinct that had been ingrained in her during the relentless battle against her father.

So, the first thing she would need to have was evidence that Mr. Bingley saw her whole self and not just her pretty face. If he could see through her mask, then her newborn hopes might just find a way to flourish. Jane also realized she would need to know with confidence that he respected her decisions and wanted what was best for her and the people that she loved.

That thought drew Jane up straight in her seat. Had last night been an inkling of his desire to do what was best for her? Granted, it was all rather hazy. Pain had prevented her from thinking of much else at the time, but she might have more hope than she had originally thought. She could not be sure, not quite yet, but if she was observant and allowed things to progress, she might soon find all that she wanted.

A soft knock at the door alerted Jane to the presence of her lady's maid. Seeing her in the chair, the woman said, "Oh, Miss Bennet, you are up. How are you feeling?"

Smiling at the sweet woman, Jane sought to reassure her. "Much better, Dawson. My megrims do not come frequently, but when they do, I often feel better with a good night's sleep and some willow bark tea. Thank you so much for all your help last night. You seemed to know just what to do."

Moving to the wardrobe, Dawson began laying out an outfit for her to wear. Jema Dawson had been her maid for less than six months, having been a gift of sorts from her brother-in-law, and Jane was delighted with how well they got along. Dawson knew her tastes and was of a cheerful disposition. Though it still felt odd to use her last name, she knew that for lady's maids, it was apparently a sign of respect.

"I am just glad you are feeling better. My younger sister had megrims every month when she got her monthlies, the poor dear, so I have a lot of experience providing ease for them." Turning to Jane with two dresses in her arms, she added, "The weather seems to be promising. Would you prefer the pink or the peach?"

Looking at the gowns, Jane fleetingly wondered if Mr. Bingley had a preference in colors. Shaking her head, she asked, "I do not know. Which do you think is most flattering?"

"You look well in both, if I may say so, but you often wear pink dresses. It is possible that the change in color might draw some attention."

"Then peach it is." Nodding her head, Jane began the routine of preparing for the day. It would be nice to spend time with Elizabeth after being apart for so long. She would also have the opportunity to study Mr. Bingley and planned to keep a watchful eye, eager to glimpse any reason to hope on that front.

Chapter Four

As he stirred his tea with his spoon, the gentle clinking went unnoticed by Bingley. Though when he glanced briefly away from the doorway and in the direction of his friend, he noticed the annoyance on Darcy's face. Promptly removing his spoon and laying it on the saucer, Bingley reflexively shrugged his shoulders. "Sorry about that. I know you hate that sound."

Briefly making a face that stemmed from years of companionship, ranging back to their adolescence, Darcy said, "I know you are worried about her, but I am sure she is well. Otherwise, I would have heard of it before now."

Leaning back in his chair, Bingley sighed and tapped his fingers on the table. Eventually he said, "While I know that, I still cannot help but worry. You are married to the woman you love and can see to her whenever the mood strikes you. I, on the other hand, must merely worry and pine."

Taking a sip of his morning coffee, Darcy raised his eyebrows and looked at Bingley in a way that he recalled from his days back at

Cambridge. Often when Bingley would struggle to study before a test, Darcy would try to help quiz him. He would regularly become frustrated when Bingley could not seem to remember things he should, in Darcy's opinion, have known. "Yes, if you recall, I had my own cause for worry as I was falling in love with her sister. So I am not unsympathetic to your plight."

Running his hand down his face, Bingley looked from the doorway to Darcy once more. "Yes, I know. I am simply out of sorts." Gaze flickering around the empty room, Bingley sat up straighter, realizing what it was that had seemed off. Mrs. Darcy was not present. "Where is your lady love? Isn't she normally as deliriously happy to rise early as you are? It is rare to see you without her by your side when not at the business of running Pemberley."

Twisting his cup back and forth on the table, Darcy's brow drew together in apparent consternation. "Yes, well, she was sleeping so soundly that I did not want to disturb her. You are correct in thinking she is normally up with the sun, but she has been sleeping more of late."

Watching his friend worry about his young wife made Bingley feel like a cad. How was that he had not noticed his friend's agitation before now? Leaning forward in his chair, Bingley sought to reassure Darcy. "I am sure she is merely adjusting to the responsibility of running an estate. A few good night's sleep is all she needs."

Smiling faintly at his friend, Darcy said, "Yes, I am sure it is something as simple as that, though I do hope she is not coming down with something."

"Who is coming down with something?"

Bingley's attention swiveled to the doorway where Jane stood. Her blue eyes were on both the men, eyebrows raised. "Your sister is sleeping in later than usual, and her husband is concerned that she may be coming down with something. I have been trying to convince him she is fine."

Tilting her head, Jane was quick to say, "I am sure she only needed some extra sleep, but even if she comes down with a spring cold, you will find there are plenty of ladies present to ensure her quick recovery. I would not worry overmuch about it, William."

Darcy nodded while Bingley hopped to his feet and pulled out the chair next to his for her. "Do sit down. I will get you some tea, unless you would prefer coffee this morning?" Looking at Jane closely, he studied her appearance, hoping to find her improved from the previous evening. Though she seemed to be only slightly paler than usual, the peach dress she wore was lovely, and Bingley was happy to see her appearing much better than the night before. The lines of pain were no longer evident, and her smile seemed genuine and certainly less brittle. "Is your head improved?"

Moving to sit down, Jane smiled at him in a way that would have caused Bingley to stumble had he been attempting to walk. "I know that I normally prefer tea, but coffee with cream and sugar sounds lovely. Thank you for your concern. My head is much improved from last night. Sometimes a good night's sleep will improve much in what ails you."

Bingley moved to the sideboard to prepare Jane her cup of coffee as she spoke. He was happy he had been correct in thinking her improved. Returning to her side, he placed the cup and saucer before her and was relieved when she smiled after her first sip. "Would you like me to make you up a plate?" he asked, grateful for the opportunity to dote on her.

Taking another sip of her coffee, she asked, "Have you gentlemen not eaten?"

"No, we have been waiting for the ladies to join us." Darcy's gaze shifted from Jane back to the doorway, almost as if he wished his wife to magically appear. "I suppose they will all come down soon enough."

Jane glanced at Bingley with an amused look before saying, "Yes, I am sure *they* will come down shortly." They turned to watch Darcy's normally stoic expression morph into a rueful blush. Smiling, Jane continued with, "I am sure Lizzie will not mind at all if you start without her."

Bingley watched as Darcy sighed, pushed back from the table, and went to the sideboard. "I suppose it is a waste to let all of this lovely food sit here and grow cold."

AFTER SHE HAD FINISHED eating and chatting with Mr. Bingley and William, Jane went in search of her sister. William had seemed to take her reassurance well enough, but that did not mean she was not also concerned for Elizabeth. There were only a few places her sister could be, and Jane made quick work of finding her.

In the end, Elizabeth sat yawning at her dressing table, and Jane actually stood watching her for some time before she was noticed. Turning, she smiled warmly at her sister. "Jane, are you feeling better?"

"Much," Jane smiled as she tilted her head and studied her younger sister carefully. Had she been unwell yesterday without Jane noticing, or did she simply have a very poor night's sleep? "Though I am now wondering how you are feeling. It is not like you to awaken after me. Are you well?"

Yawing again, Elizabeth shook herself like a dog shaking water off its back. "I simply cannot get moving this morning. Things have been relatively calm, and I slept well, but I am dragging today, and I cannot understand why." Glancing back to herself in the mirror, Elizabeth poked at her cheek, apparently taking in her pallid complexion.

Walking over to Elizabeth, Jane took up the brush and began running it through her sister's wild locks. It was a soothing action for them both, going back to a time before either of them had a lady's maid and they took turns caring for each other. "Whatever this is, I am sure you will be well served to have a hearty breakfast. I think Mother and our sisters will be in the dining room, unless you want to eat up here?"

"No, I will go down. I know William is most likely worried about me, and it is not as if I am actually ill, only exceedingly tired." Elizabeth punctuated her comment with another exceptional yawn.

Then, with a determined set of her shoulders, Elizabeth stood and linked her arm with Jane's, and together they descended the stairs.

As they made their way down, Jane wondered what their mother would think of Elizabeth's lack of energy. It was very unlike her younger sister, but Jane refused to be concerned. There were, after all, plenty of simple possibilities, at least one of which was rather positive.

Breakfast was a jolly affair, with all the sisters chatting merrily over eggs, sausage, and various baked goods. Jane enjoyed a second cup of coffee while everyone ate and chatted. She shared a look with her mother, full of implication. It seemed that they both were developing suspicions about Elizabeth.

It was always interesting for Jane to note how in tune her mother seemed to be with all of her daughters. With a few glances, they could share their concern for Elizabeth, as well as their suspicions. Jane noticed when Elizabeth took a second helping of sausage but turned her nose up at coffee and instead asked for tea with sugar and no cream. There was definitely something going on.

"Mr. Bingley!"

A familiar small voice grabbed Bingley's attention and, turning around, he spotted Kiernan hurrying in his direction. He had come to know the courageous boy during the whole escapade back in Meryton. Bingley studied the boy as he approached on the well-worn path that traversed the Pemberley's kitchen gardens. Carefully dodging a plant that Bingley was unfamiliar with, Kiernan practically skipped over to him. Kiernan hadn't seemed to have lost any of his enthusiasm, if his grin was any indication, though he had shot up in height.

Greeting him with a smile, Bingley said, "Kiernan, it has been a while. How are you and your family?"

Kiernan's intelligent brown eyes sparkled as he nodded his head. "They are well. Thank you for asking."

Bingley still felt vaguely guilty whenever he looked into the boy's kind face. It was only too easy for him to still remember the bruising on his cheek. The memories of the previous autumn flooded back, reminding him of his sister's cruel actions when she not only struck the boy but also forcibly expelled him from Netherfield. It had been the event that finally spurred him into action. He not only allocated Caroline's pin money for the quarter into an account for the boy, but he also reached out to his Aunt Guthrie for support. In the end, it had been the very best thing—Caroline had spent the winter with their aunt in Scotland and was much better for it.

"I am glad." Bingley was truly relieved that Kiernan seemed to be adjusting to the move from Longbourn. Darcy had offered a home to any families that had felt the need to flee Mr. Bennet's grasp, and Kiernan's family had been the first to accept. "Do you like the home farm?"

Bouncing eagerly on his toes as he spoke, Kiernan answered, "Yes! Not only do I have my own room and get to help with the cows, but my whole family is also glad. Though I must admit that I am especially fond of the tutor Mr. Darcy has arranged for me. I get to take lessons three days a week."

Bingley laughed. "I was never nearly as enthusiastic about learning as you seem to be. I was always more interested in other things, like running about being a pirate or fishing, or trying to get my father to let me ride a horse."

Looking over towards the stables, Kiernan added, "Oh, I like horses too. That is why I came early so I could say hello to Crumpet and his friends before I meet with Mr. Johnson, my tutor."

Patting him on the shoulder, Bingley said, "Then I will not stop you. The poor horse might go into a decline if he misses your visit."

Kiernan gave a little bow and then jogged off to visit the noble horse that he called a friend. It still tickled Bingley that the boy was so fond of the nickname that Georgianna had given the extra-large horse. At least Cadmus seemed accepting of the name Crumpet and the affection that Kiernan lavished on him.

Watching the boy disappear into the building, Bingley remembered what he had been about before he became distracted. Taking a well-worn path around the outside of Pemberley, Bingley made his way to the kitchen gardens. He knew Jane often spent mornings either in the still room or in the garden caring for the medicinal herbs.

While Bingley had agreed to accompany Darcy to inspect the fields that were to be readied for planting in an hour, that did not mean he had to sit around and wait to leave. He had already changed into work clothes and still he had more time on his hands. He felt compelled to seek out Miss Bennet's presence for all that he had no idea what he might say to her. After only a few more steps, Bingley's hopes were rewarded, and his anxiety multiplied. He had hoped to come up with what he wanted to say on the way to finding her, but so far, he did not know what words should come out of his mouth.

"Mr. Bingley, you startled me," Jane spoke with her hand on her chest. She had been so focused on weeding around the chamomile bed that she hadn't heard him approach. It was growing well, but it would still be some time before harvesting any. The feverfew in the bed nearby was especially prolific and might be ready to work with soon.

Clearing his throat, Mr. Bingley said, "I am sorry to disturb you. I was…just going to say hello."

Jane watched Mr. Bingley blush slightly and rub at his furrowed brow with a single finger. The poor man truly did try. "No harm done, Mr. Bingley. I was paying more attention to my herbs than to my surroundings."

"Darcy went to check on Mrs. Darcy. Do you know if she is well?" Scuffing the ground with the toe of his boot, Bingley looked at Jane with eyebrows raised.

Jane nodded while putting down a handful of weeds and replied, "Yes, I think she is. She might just need more time to rest. Unless anything else develops, I do not think we should worry." Tilting her head, Jane considered his hopeful yet lost expression. She had decided just that morning that she wanted to discern whether he looked merely at her appearance or whether he recognized her true self. In order to do that, she would have to spend time with him. Maybe it would give her the opportunity to see him in action, so to speak. It would not be a struggle, for she rather enjoyed his company. With a smile, she asked, "Would you like to help me with my herbs?"

"I would love to be of use." Kneeling on a mat adjacent to Jane, he appeared to study the vibrant new growth before him. Turning his gaze back to her, he inquired, "What are you cultivating here?"

Running a delicate finger along the spine of one of the plants, Jane's smile widened. It always felt as if she were spending time with old companions when she worked in the garden. Turning to Mr. Bingley, she explained, "This is chamomile. It makes a lovely tea, but I prefer to use it in compresses for inflammation or rashes. Over there is feverfew which, as you might guess, is helpful in fighting fevers. It also helps with megrims."

Mr. Bingley turned out to be an enthusiastic student, willing to get his hands dirty and follow her direction. He was humble enough to listen to her willingly, without hesitation or the desire to show her up. Her father never would have been disposed to work and get his hands dirty or listen to her mother's directions. Jane was grateful for the company and more than happy to tick one thing off her list.

FINDING HIS WIFE HAD been a simple matter of checking a few of her favorite rooms. Darcy really was worried about her unusual exhaustion, though perhaps it was not exhaustion. She was not necessarily that level of tired, but still, he was worried. He had never seen her this tired before. Spotting her at a window in one of the upstairs sitting rooms, he came up behind Elizabeth, and looked over her shoulder to see what she was observing with such interest. Down below in the herb garden, Jane and Bingley were working with the plants. It seemed like they were enjoying themselves, though Darcy could not be certain from this distance.

An enormous grin crept across his face, tempting his dimples to come into play. His poor wife wanted his friend and her sister to realize how perfect they were for each other so badly. Darcy leaned over and put his chin on his wife's shoulder. "I never would have thought to catch you spying on your sister." Laughing faintly, he added, "You should come away from the window, Elizabeth. Spying on them will not help them along."

Leaning back into his muscular figure, Elizabeth sighed. "I only want them to be as happy as we are."

"You cannot force things, my love. Everything will progress or not as it should." Darcy wrapped his arms around Elizabeth, holding her to him. He was glad to be able to spend some time alone with her. He could not help asking, "Are you sure you are all right?"

Turning in the circle of his arms, Elizabeth turned her back on the window and gazed into Darcy's eyes. Then, leaning up on tiptoes, she kissed his cheek. "Yes, I am fine. I was just unusually tired. I would let you know if there was something to worry about." Settling back into his arms, her head in the crook of his neck, Elizabeth hummed under her breath.

Darcy closed his eyes, savoring the connection they shared. He was not entirely sure that his wife would tell him if there was something wrong. She was always trying to look out for him and would not want him to worry, in her opinion, *needlessly*. He would have to keep a close eye on her, but for now, he would simply enjoy having her in his arms.

Chapter Five

MRS. BENNET LOOKED AROUND the room at all her merry girls, and of course she included Georgianna in the number. Spring was always a busy time on the estate. Fields were being readied for planting, and the farms would soon be overrun with new little lambs and calves. Things seem to be progressing apace. The ladies of Pemberley were primarily concerned with more mundane things, like the health of the tenants and the need for baby clothes and blankets.

"I cannot convey just how adorable the new colt is, all clumsy legs and spirit. You will all have to go down and see it," Lydia spoke, her face shining with excitement as she worked her knitting needles at a fast-clicking pace.

Looking up from the small desk in the corner where she was writing, Elizabeth asked, "Does the colt look anything like Cadmus?"

Tilting her head, Lydia paused in her knitting in apparent thought before finally describing him, "He is dark like his sire, but has a splash of color on his forehead. As gangly as he is at this point, it is hard for me to picture him as a great strong beast like Cadmus, but who knows, anything is possible."

Fanny could not help but look at her energetic daughter with fondness. Of all her daughters, Lydia seemed the least affected by having grown up in an oppressive environment. She was almost always enthusiastic about what she was interested in, whether that be her love of children, flowers, or the latest colt in the stable.

Georgianna bit off a piece of thread and held the little garment out in front of her, smiling at her work for a moment. Laying the garment down, she leaned over and began searching through the basket beside her, commenting, "I am sure William will be happy that he has another male from Crumpet's line. He is an exemplary horse." The more she searched in the basket next to her, the deeper the furrow on her forehead became, a sign of her increasing perplexity. "I thought we had more little ribbons. I was hoping to add some pretty bits for this gown."

Jane looked up from her own needlework and said, "I think we have used up most of our little odds and ends. What were you making?" Leaning over, she looked at the little gown that lay on Georgianna's lap.

Smoothing the gown out, Georgianna smiled softly as Jane admired her work. With a blush, she said, "Oh, it is nothing much, just a little gown for one of the babies we are expecting this spring. In the coming months, three tenant families are expecting babies, and I want to make each of them a little outfit and cap. I just wanted them to have something a little special. You know how many hand-me-downs these children inherit."

"Every child deserves something nice, and every mother loves to dress their child nicely. Your little gown will be well appreciated, Georgie." Setting down her own work—a pair of baby booties—Mrs. Bennet smiled and added, "I propose we take the carriage into Lambton later today. We can restock our supplies, and maybe even visit the bookshop and tearoom."

Fanny watched as the girls all started excitedly chatting about the trip. It appeared that her suggestion was well received. Watching their animated faces, Fanny smiled. They were such good girls; it was so nice to see them all at ease and busily working on projects that they enjoyed.

Lydia clapped her hands with a soft laugh. "Brilliant! I am sure that we can find all the little bits of ribbon and the like at the shops there."

Mary was quick to join in the merriment. Reaching over, she clasped Georgianna's arm. "What do you think of looking for new sheet music, Georgianna? Perhaps we could find a new duet to work on."

Watching Kitty chat excitedly about a paint set and canvas with Elizabeth and Jane, Fanny mused that the enthusiasm of six women offered the chance to go shopping could not be suppressed. Nodding her head, Fanny had to raise her voice to be heard above the enthusiastic chatter. "It is settled—we will go to Lambton."

Riding next to Darcy, Bingley looked over the land, appreciating the view. They were approaching a quaint two-story building built on a slight rise. There were cows in the yard and a smattering of chickens. Something about the scene felt comforting in a way that Bingley had not expected. "Is there a problem with the home farm?" asked Bingley.

Shaking his head, Darcy said, "No, not really. I just wanted to check in with the Andersons. They are one of the families that have come from Longbourn, and I have been trying to make sure that they have all that they need."

Bingley was curious to hear how the families that had been so misused by Mr. Bennet were fairing. Looking over at his friend on his dark steed, Cadmus, he asked, "How has everyone settled in?"

"For the most part, very well." Darcy seemed to consider his words for a moment before further saying, "I do not think they are at all used to being checked on by a gentleman. I do not think Mr. Bennet ever saw to their needs back at Longbourn. They are more accustomed to Elizabeth or her sisters checking on them and trying to cobble a solution together if there is an issue. So, they usually seem uneasy when I arrive."

Tilting his head, Bingley considered what Darcy had said. "Mr. Bennet couldn't care less about anyone but himself. It seems as if everything he touched is suffering from his involvement or lack thereof."

JANE LOOKED AROUND THE bookshop for her mother and the rest of her sisters. Kitty and Lydia were still back at their favorite shop looking over ribbons, and she was all too aware that Elizabeth would lose track of time when surrounded by books. Normally, her mother was good at keeping track of the time and their schedule, but it was past time for them to meet up and walk over to the teashop.

Jane had already bought the supplies they needed for the still room. They had been running low on powdered willow bark and ginger, and she was glad they had an ample supply to augment Pemberley's stores. Jane always felt uneasy if she was running low on willow bark, as it was always needed for spring colds and fevers. As for ginger, it had many uses, even if what she suspected was not the case.

It was a good thing the store was not excessively large, as it would make her wayward family easier to find. She spotted Mary and Georgianna immediately by the window, looking at sheet music. Proceeding around the corner of a row of shelves, Jane went to the back of the shop, thinking she would spot Elizabeth near the works of Shakespeare or animal husbandry. Her sister was indeed a peculiar woman in her tastes.

Her expectation to find Elizabeth left her rather surprised when she came across her mother talking with William's neighbor, Mr. Hawkins. Not only was her mother chatting happily with the man about who knows what, her eyes were sparkling. In her almost twenty-two years, Jane could not ever remember her mother ever looking like that. As if she was happy and carefree and enjoying a moment in the sun after a long, desolate winter.

Frozen in place, Jane had no idea how to react to what was before her. A gentle tug at her elbow had Jane turning to look at Elizabeth, who gestured to follow her into a nearby alcove. When she deemed them far enough away, her strangled whisper burst forth, "How long has that been going on?"

Elizabeth shrugged. "They have been talking for quite some time. I suspect this is not the first time they have encountered each other."

Jane struggled to keep her mouth from dropping open in shock. "But Mama is still married. How—" Snapping her mouth shut and tightly pursing her lips, Jane shook her head. She did not even know how to finish that sentence.

Eyes narrowing at her, Elizabeth huffed. "I do not think that is something she has forgotten. She would never behave improperly." Then, peeking through a gap in the books on the shelf, she watched their mother for a moment. Turning back to Jane, she said, "I cannot begrudge her a friend."

Jane sighed, understanding for the first time how lonely their mother must be. "No, you are right. Mother would never allow things to progress too far."

"Besides, William says with the rate our father is falling into drink and disreputable behavior, Mama might not be married for very much longer."

This was information that Jane had not heard before. When they had fled Longbourn, she had tried to put it and her father out of her mind. Jane leaned closer to her sister and asked, "What do you know?"

Glancing around, Elizabeth made sure they were not going to be overheard before leaning in and whispering, "William has had people watching father; he wants to be aware if he tries to cause problems for us." Elizabeth waited for Jane to show her understanding before continuing, her voice low and almost hesitant. "Father has gone bankrupt and was recently forced to leave Longbourn. He has had to search for employment, but you and I both know that he is too insolent and lazy to hold any worthwhile position. His lodgings are in a very seedy part of town, and William has learned that he has offended several people who do not like to be crossed. Between his drinking and his behavior, I truly doubt our father is long for this world."

Jane knew she must look odd, with her eyes wide and her mouth in a startled 'o,' but she could barely wrangle her mind into a rational pattern of thought. How should she feel about that information? She believed a dutiful daughter would feel sorrow knowing that her father was suffering, but Jane could not find it in herself to do so. Too many years of his cruelty, not only towards herself but the mother and sisters whom she loved, had eroded any feeling of compassion she might have had for him. Was it at all correct to be feeling relief that she might be able to put her father behind her once and for all? Would she finally feel liberated when he was gone? Or was it possible that it was too late, and her experiences had already made her who she was, for better or worse?

Elizabeth reached out and squeezed Jane's hand, offering her sister silent support. Eventually, she asked, "Did you get everything you needed from the various shops?"

Nodding her head, Jane managed to bring her mind out of her ponderings. "Yes, though Kitty and Lydia are both still admiring all the ribbons."

"Then let us gather everyone and walk to the teashop. I think we could both do with a cup." Linking arms with Jane as they had often done when they were younger, Elizabeth called out to her mother, saying that they were going to the teashop.

Jane let her sisters' chatter wash over her as she walked down the stairs on the way down to dinner. The trip into town had been the highlight of Kitty and Lydia's week, and while Mary and Georgianna were less effusive of their joy, they still spoke softly about practicing their duet after dinner. Though she was happy that her sisters were happy, Jane was still disturbed by what she had learned of her father's situation.

She knew that people often thought she was often too forgiving of others. Jane made a conscious effort to see the best in people, striving to forgive their mistakes and accept their flaws. There was, however, a line past which she found it hard to forgive. When someone hurt the people she cared for, Jane reacted as harshly as it was in her ability to do so. Thankfully, she had encountered very few people who were foolish enough to hurt those closest to her. Her father, however, was at the top of her list of those people.

Jane struggled with forgiveness when it came to him. She was displeased with the negative emotions of anger and animosity that had accumulated within her in regard to her father. It was one of the reasons she forgave so freely; she did not like carrying that weight in her heart. The news that a person she knew had fallen on hard times would normally tug at her heartstrings, instantly prompting her to find a way to go to their aid. With her father, it was another story.

She had tried to forget about him as much as possible and had been fairly successful. Focusing on rebuilding her life away from Longbourn had helped. Watching her sisters and even her mother bloom as they adapted to living at Pemberley had helped even more. Seeing their happiness had led to her own happiness and just when she was growing content and comfortable in her new home, her father had crept back into her life.

She absolutely hated the fear that settled into her veins simply upon hearing about him. She hated the way he made her feel, and she hated him, and more than that, she hated that he had pushed her as far as hatred.

Despite all those feelings rolling through her like a turbulent ocean, Jane put a small smile on her face and averted her eyes from her sisters' gazes. She did not want to worry them about her discontent. Jane knew that she would find a way to work through it all. She always did. That is what she told herself. But then, as she came to the bottom of the stairs, she was greeted by Mr. Bingley.

He had let her sisters pass him up and waited for her with his arm extended. "Miss Bennet, you look beautiful tonight."

Jane could literally feel her ire rising. She detested that word when it was applied to herself. Babies were beautiful, her sisters were beautiful, and anything that Kitty created was beautiful, but she hated to hear people say that she was beautiful. She was so much more than her appearance. She had thought Mr. Bingley might appreciate her for herself and not merely for her outer appearance.

Flashing him a smile that she knew did not reach her eyes, Jane accepted his escort, but did not say a word. She was already in a bad mood and was struggling to maintain her happy veneer. As if she didn't have enough to contend with, his unfortunate statement added to the weight she carried in her ongoing struggle to appear serene.

BINGLEY HATED TO ADMIT it, but he was frustrated. Most people might believe that he was always cheerful and sociable and, for the most part, he was, or at least he tried to be. That did not prevent him from sometimes wanting to think and, even at times, brood. At that moment, he was leaning towards brooding. Sitting alone in his guest room, staring at the flickering flames in the fireplace, Bingley wondered where he had gone wrong.

He had been at Pemberley for over a week, and he thought his pursuit of Jane had been going well. Though maybe pursuit was not the correct word, but he did not exactly know what word suited better. He had been trying to prove to her that he was worthy of her trust, and to show her he loved her. Maybe even demonstrate to her he would treat her well and she would be safe in his care. Bingley strongly suspected that with a father like hers, she must be terrified of becoming linked to a man unworthy of her love.

Though Jane had gone with him into the dining room, she had said not a word. Bingley knew her smile was just the facade she wore when she did not want to show her genuine emotions. His Jane never frowned, not outright, but her eyes were shadowed, and when she looked at him, they had seemed cold.

He thought it had been working. Jane had seemed truly happy with his attention. Somehow, it had all been upset, and he did not know how or why. What could he have done to receive such a cold shoulder at dinner? Was it something he had said or done?

Bingley restrained the desire to find a hard surface that he could bang his head against. Instead, he forced himself to think back to the moment when he realized things were going wrong. Jane had been coming down the stairs, and he noticed she did not look quite herself. He had thought that he might perk her up by offering a compliment. That was the exact moment when things had started to go downhill.

All he had said was that she looked beautiful. Most woman wanted to be called beautiful. Was it possible that Jane did not? He knew it was something she probably heard a lot. Her beauty was the first thing people noticed when she was in London. He could not go five feet without other men singing odes to her classic beauty. All their talk was one of the reasons he had not wanted to spend more time in London. He could not abide watching all the superficial gentlemen fawn over her.

Was it possible that she had not liked it any more than he did? Was that the reason why she left London so early? Should he apologize for calling her beautiful? It was not a lie, nor was it an insult, but it was becoming clear that she might feel it was.

He would have to refrain from calling attention to her physical beauty. Indeed, she possessed many other qualities that he valued. Sighing, he rested his head in his hand. This evening had definitely been a setback, but there was always tomorrow.

Chapter Six

Lydia knocked on her sister's door but did not wait for her answer to enter. There were benefits to being the youngest of a group of sisters—she found she managed to get away with quite a lot. Not that she ever truly tried to misbehave, she just tested the boundaries of what her sisters found acceptable. What did it matter if she went into their rooms uninvited or borrowed bonnets without asking? She was the baby. Everyone loved her.

She found Jane sitting by the fireplace, staring at the flames. For a moment, before her sister realized she was there, Lydia spotted a rare frown on Jane's face and was able to read her true level of unhappiness.

Then, in a blink, Jane's smile was in place, and she turned to greet her. "Lydia, did you need something, dear?"

Lydia tilted her head as she watched Jane and moved to lean against the chair across from where her oldest sister sat. "I was wondering why you turned so cold towards Mr. Bingley at dinner. Did he do something to upset you?"

Jane's smile never slipped, but Lydia watched as her eyes widened and her eyebrows rose. Lydia had learned a while back that watching her sister's eyes was the key to deciphering her actual emotions. She waited patiently for Jane to respond. She had a feeling that she might be the only sister who might be able to get away with questioning Jane without being immediately shut down. For all that she was close to Lizzie, Lizzie was too respectful of Jane's boundaries. Lydia, on the other hand, was fond of crossing boundaries.

"I was perfectly civil at dinner. Everything is fine. You do not need to worry," came Jane's calm response.

"While you might have been civil, you were by no means happy or as warm as you normally are. In fact, you were decidedly cold towards Mr. Bingley."

Jane looked away from Lydia and back into the fire. Silence lingered in the air, creating an uneasy tension, before Jane finally broke it by saying, "I am sorry if I worried you. I was merely preoccupied with something."

Flopping herself into the chair inelegantly over the arm, Lydia replied, "I can read you, you know." Sometimes it was fun to go against the rules of being a proper lady. Once she could tell she had Jane's full attention, she added, "I am not such a child anymore. I can tell the difference between distracted and upset and anger. You were angry tonight at dinner. In fact, I think you were upset even before dinner, but something between you and Mr. Bingley made it worse."

Jane's head shot up at those words and Lydia could see her gaze sharpen. She knew she had hit a nerve when Jane said, "I am only having an off evening. Besides, I doubt he could tell. People who are not my family are rarely able to decipher my moods."

Lydia sighed and sat up in her chair correctly. Lydia knew her sister and Mr. Bingley had feelings for one another, but something was keeping them apart. She suspected it was Jane who was keeping things moving at a crawl. She could tell that it was hurting Mr. Bingley, and worse, it was hurting Jane. It was time to turn the screws, so to speak. She did not want Jane stuck being miserable when she could very well be happy. Lydia looked Jane right in the eye and said, "Mr. Bingley has stayed with the family after dinner every evening, but this evening, he made up an excuse and went to bed early. I do believe that he noticed and was, in fact, hurt by your behavior."

JANE CLOSED HER EYES at her sister's words. Lydia was right—Mr. Bingley had been able to tell. He had left to go to his room, and despite her cold behavior, Mr. Bingley had not once said or done anything that was ungenerous. She had hurt him, had distanced herself from him, and he had not completely deserved it.

Jane did not want to go into her feelings about their father with Lydia, but she felt she did need to explain herself to a certain extent. So before she could lose courage, Jane opened her eyes and blurted, "He called me *beautiful*."

Lydia's reaction was not what Jane had expected. Then again, Lydia was not what many people expected. Lydia laughed and said,

"I am sorry, Jane, but you are, in fact, beautiful. There is no avoiding it." Then, after laughing some more, she became serious and said, "As I do not see him going blind in the near future, if you want him to not comment on it, you will need to explain matters to him."

It was odd watching Lydia, her little sister, counsel her. Lydia rarely struck her as a serious person. She was the sister most likely to flop in her chair sideways or laugh at inappropriate moments. It seemed, though, that as she was growing up, she had a serious, logical side. "But it sounds so ridiculous out loud."

Lydia shrugged. "If he is the man for you like I think he is, then he will understand. If he doesn't understand, then he is not the man for you. Either way, he does not deserve to be penalized for saying something that every other woman in the world would be flattered by." Getting up, Lydia gave Jane a kiss on the cheek and turned to go.

Jane responded with a murmur. "I know. I just wish he saw the person I am inside."

From the door, Lydia turned and asked, "How do you know he doesn't?" Lydia's words landed on Jane's conscience like a sudden, forceful slap, causing her to almost miss her sister's next comment. "Good night, Jane. Do not stay up all night worrying." Then, with a soft click of the door, she was gone.

Leaning back in her chair, Jane sighed and resumed watching the flames. Now she felt upset and guilty. Lydia was right, though. She should not judge Mr. Bingley when he did not have all the information he needed. He had no way of knowing how she would react to that word.

But how to bring up that kind of conversation? "Mr. Bingley, you may have noticed that I reacted badly the other night when you called me beautiful. I hate that word, so please refrain from calling me that, and everything should go smoothly." No, that just seemed wrong somehow. Eventually, Jane gave up trying to find a way to bring up such an awkward topic and went to bed. She knew that it was not a problem that would magically vanish on its own, but she was tired and needed sleep. It was a problem for another day.

By morning, Bingley had decided he could not become bogged down with discouragement. So it was with a determined heart that he got ready for the day. He would see Jane, but he would not let her pique from the night before upset his efforts. He had known going into the situation that he had an uphill battle. Experience had shown him that patience and reliability were key when it came to most things. Hopefully, they would also be the key to winning Jane's trust. Somehow, he knew that he already had her love. It was odd to see both love and conflict in her eyes when he looked at her. He wasn't fighting just to win her heart, but also her mind, her trust, and her belief in the hope of triumphing over her past.

Thinking back, he remembered the dog he had adopted as a young boy of nine. She had been the most beautiful little thing that he had named Belle. Not a purebred dog, she had been some mix of breeds that had left her with a unique cream and gray coat. Though they had ended up being the best of friends, it had not started out that way.

When he had first discovered the dog, it was obvious that she had been mistreated. The first time Bingley had seen her timid tail wag, he had fallen in love, and he had been determined that they would be the best of friends. It had taken him some time to gain the dog's trust, and why wouldn't it? It had taken time and experience to taint her faith in humanity and goodness. Even that long ago, he had understood that it would take time to build both concepts back up. He had not given up, despite the time it took for Belle to grow to love him. Eventually, his efforts had borne fruit in a dog who loved him back just as powerfully as he loved her.

Rolling his eyes at his own thoughts, Bingley left his room and walked towards the stairs. Jane was not a dog, and it was probably wrong to compare her to Belle, but somehow the situations felt the same. Jane had genuine reasons to be hesitant about a relationship with him. He admitted to himself that until he met the Bennet ladies, he had never realized how cruel someone could be to their family, or for that matter, the precarious situations women often found themselves in.

He would carry on with his usual demeanor, remaining true to himself. In every circumstance, he would be by Jane's side, providing his loyalty and proving that he was not vindictive or unkind. He had enough confidence in them as a couple for the both of them for now.

It was only a matter of time before he would prove himself to her. Smiling to himself, Bingley walked into the morning room and went to the sideboard to get himself a cup of coffee.

A startled "Oh" had Bingley turning to see Jane standing in the doorway. As always, his eyes drank her in like a thirsty man. Every hair was in place, but her normally glowing skin was a touch paler than usual. Concern led him to examine her appearance more closely. The pale blue dress she wore brought out the blue in her eyes but also drew attention to how red they were. It didn't take long for Bingley to deduce that she must have had a restless night.

Smiling kindly, he said, "Good morning, Miss Bennet. Would you like for me to fetch you some coffee or tea?"

Bingley watched Jane sigh and then smile. "Good morning, Mr. Bingley. Coffee would be lovely. Thank you." It seemed to Bingley that her smile was genuine, if tired.

Abandoning the idea of his own coffee in favor of getting hers, Bingley added a good amount of cream and one lump of sugar to her cup. Delivering it to Jane, he waited until she took a sip and smiled at his work before going to get his own cup. Sitting down at the table across from Jane with his cup of coffee, he fortified himself with the potent brew.

Should he speak first? Come up with something random? What should he say? He had been so focused on coming up with some form of benign chatter that he almost missed it when Jane started speaking.

JANE WATCHED CHARLES SIP his coffee, trying to gather the courage to say what she knew she must say. She had gone to sleep struggling to determine the words she should use to apologize and try to explain herself. It had been a fruitless endeavor. Despite the ideal circumstances for an apology, she found herself unable to articulate her thoughts.

Could she just apologize? Would that work? It might, and it was the only idea that she had. Clearing her throat, she said, "Mr. Bingley, I would like to apologize for my behavior last night. I have realized that my behavior could be seen as rude or, in Lydia's words, cruel." As Jane spoke, she couldn't bring herself to meet Mr. Bingley's gaze, fearing the pain she might see. Guilt eventually forced her to look up. If there was pain in his eyes, she deserved to see it. She had put it there, after all. As she studied his blue eyes, pain wasn't the only thing she saw—she also saw hope.

"You were having a bad evening. I would never dream of holding that against you. I would go so far as to say you do not need to apologize, but it is obvious that your apology is important to you." Putting his cup down, he fidgeted with it for a moment before tightening his lips in a grim smile. "I too want to offer an apology."

Leaning forward, Jane said, "No, I was at fault last night. I am sorry if you feel as if—" Jane stopped her protest when she noted the look on Mr. Bingley's face. His smile had disappeared, and now he actually looked pained.

Mr. Bingley slowly reached out and lay his hand over hers where it rested on the table. "You cannot deny that something I said last night hurt you."

Jane closed her eyes. She could only feel the warmth of his hand on hers. It took her a moment to open her eyes and find the ability to whisper, "No, I cannot deny it, but that is more my problem than yours."

Squeezing her hand, Bingley said, "But I want to make it my problem. What did I say that hurt you?"

"You said that I was *beautiful*." Jane looked down at her cup and watched the steam rise off the dark liquid.

"And that upset you?" Hearing his question, Jane gazed back at Mr. Bingley. He did not react to her statement as she had thought he would. She had thought he would think her ridiculous, but it was apparent that was not the case.

Reassured by his response, Jane only hesitated briefly before saying, "I must admit that it is something I have heard more than I would like and often from men who care for little else than my physical appearance."

HE HAD KNOWN THAT something he said had set her off, but to hear that it was calling her beautiful hurt. Not that he was insulted. No, he ached because he knew how much she was hurting from the shallowness she encountered. It was a cruel world they lived in that something that should have been a lovely compliment could be misused and thus become painful.

Bingley believed her father had inflicted the initial wound, using her beauty as a weapon to hurt her, cutting her confidence like a knife. He would simply have to prove himself. Waiting until her gaze locked onto his, he said, "I could tell you that I appreciate all that you are, but that would only be words, and you deserve more than pretty words. Would you give me the chance to continue to prove myself to you?"

"I think I would like that." Jane faltered, biting her lip a moment before saying, "I am sorry that it is so hard for me to trust."

At least she did not say it was hard for her to trust him specifically, only in general. Bingley thought he could work with that. Shaking his head, he said, "You are only granting me my wish to pamper you, as you have always deserved to be pampered." As he spoke those daring words, Bingley could feel his cheeks grow warm. He longed to pamper Jane, but the words slipped out unintentionally at that moment, without him even realizing it. Clearing his throat, he moved past his slight embarrassment and added, "Though I must apologize now if I slip and call you beautiful. As much as you hate to hear it, I am not blind. Is there a word you might prefer I use instead? Pretty and glorious don't appeal to me much. What do you think of passable, or possibly tolerable?"

Jane's eyes lit up like he had hoped they would. He would much rather see her happy than subdued. It was a loss when she took her hand back and took a sip of her coffee, but he was willing to let her go if it meant he could see that look in her eyes. Her blue gaze held joy and a glimmer of something else. It was a look that gave him hope. Then, to top that off, she offered him a genuine smile. "Are you trying to take a page from William's book? He called Lizzie tolerable, if I do recall."

Leaning back into his chair, Bingley pretended to have trouble thinking back to the previous autumn. Tapping his finger on his chin, he finally sat up and said, "I recall him saying he could not tolerate dancing. You know how he is around crowds."

With a narrowing of her eyes, Jane seemed apt to play along, her smile morphing into a grin. "Yes, but the gossip was that he called her tolerable and not handsome enough to dance with," she countered.

Stopping to take a gulp of his coffee, he bought himself some time before he said, "Whatever he said, it worked. They are happily married and deeply in love. Why not copy an obvious example of success?" Bingley delighted in the soft blush that crept across Jane's cheeks as she took in his implication.

Bingley did not want tête-à-tête to end, but he knew it would. He could hear Lydia and Georgianna laughing as they came down the stairs. He could tell the moment that Jane realized their moment alone was nearly at an end. Raising her cup to her lips, she whispered, "I have always been fond of the effort of working towards success."

Chapter Seven

IT HAD TAKEN SOME time for Jane to become accustomed to driving the dogcart, but now she enjoyed it. Pemberley was so much larger than Longbourn had been that it was impossible to check on the tenants on foot. At first, she had tried riding to the various homes on one of the mares that Darcy kept, but she soon found that she could not carry what she needed to with her.

Thus, she had started using the dogcart. It was easier to transport food and supplies that way. At the moment, though, she had nothing left to dispense. Everyone she had seen today had sick members of their family. There was definitely something going around, and she had quickly run out of the medicine she had brought.

On a normal day, Jane would decide who to visit, maybe two or three families, and then return to Pemberley. This was not a normal day. She was concerned about finding so many people sick. The Russell family was the last on her list, and what she found made her glad that she had come. Mrs. Russell had been run off her feet, exhausted, caring for all her ill family. Her husband, oldest son, and daughter were confined to bed with how unwell they were. Her two little ones had been trying to help, but at five and three, there was not much they could do. Mary Russell had been afraid to leave them to go to Lambton for supplies, so Jane had sent the footman who went with her to the homes back to Pemberley for medicine and provisions.

When Mrs. Russell mentioned that she was concerned for the McGregor family, Jane knew that she would have to check on them before she returned to Pemberley. Apparently, they had become ill before the Russells, and though they were normally out and about, no one had seen or heard from them. So here she was, making her way to the McGregor farm. She had met them before and had found them to be quite nice.

The trail was pleasant, providing easy transport and lovely views, but Jane's mind was not on the scenery. Her mind kept wandering back to Mr. Bingley. It had been two weeks since that conversation with Mr. Bingley over breakfast, and it still hovered in the forefront of her mind. It was as if that one conversation had opened a door between them to allow for their relationship to develop more fully. She had slowly come to understand that he was the kind of man that she had been hoping for.

He had more than proven himself equal to her list of requirements and had shown on several occasions capable of seeing her through the mask she wore. Mr. Bingley had completely surprised her by knowing how much pain she had been in that first night. None of the other dandies who had been interested in her would have seen it. They could not even tell when she was unhappy with their actions, and yet Charles had seen her pain.

They had spent much time together in recent weeks, and now she found herself missing him when his responsibilities called him away, or he was helping William with some matter or another. He had been willing to assist her with the herb garden, getting dirty, planting seedlings and, to all appearances, he enjoyed it. Her father never would have done something with her mother just to be in her presence.

More than that, he had been respectful of her decisions. She knew that he loved her, and despite his feelings that were so obvious to her and basically everyone, he never pushed her to return his affection. He was allowing her the time to come to know her own feelings and build her courage, something Jane decided she was going to need in abundance. Though she was finally coming to terms with the fact that Mr. Bingley was the man of her dreams, it had not lessened her fear of voluntarily putting herself under a man's power.

To be fair, Mr. Bingley was not just any man—he was her ideal man. He had proven himself to her, and now it was her turn. She would have to find a way to show him that she was receptive to his feelings, that she was willing to marry him. Jane was not the kind of girl who could easily break convention. She would not ask him to marry her. Was there a way to encourage him to ask her?

Shaking her head, Jane admitted that her confusion was all her own fault. She had been hesitant for so long that she was unsure of how to move forward. Setting her shoulders, Jane decided it was a problem for another time. She had a family to see to. She would simply have to fret later. Turning down the lane that would take her directly to the McGregor home, she welcomed the more pleasant thoughts as she considered how they were such a lovely family.

They were a family of six—Mr. and Mrs. McGregor and their three small children, as well as Mr. McGregor's widowed mother. Jane only hoped that they were not as badly off as the Russell family. They had always been so kind and grateful when she had visited. Though they were always careful to say they had been well taken care of by Mr. Darcy in the past, the personal touch of Mrs. Darcy and her sisters coming to visit had a blessing for them.

Hopping down from her conveyance, Jane looked around the yard with concern. Things were visibly not being taken care of. The water trough was empty, and a chicken was pecking at it in frustration. It was customary for Jane to be warmly welcomed upon her arrival, but this time, things took a different turn. Feeling an uneasy terror settle into her stomach, Jane called out, "Mercy? Mr. McGregor?"

Nothing. Listening carefully, Jane tried to work up the courage to go into the house, knowing deep inside that something was horribly wrong. That was when she heard the plaintive crying, and her feet moved towards the sound.

It was worse than she could have possibly imagined.

The little kitchen area was empty of people but full of dirty clutter, and the smell of decay hung in the air. The stove had long ago gone cold, and there were a number of dirty pots in the small work area with congealed and moldy remains of food. Flies buzzed dully on the edge of her awareness as she continued further into the house, searching for the weak cry. There were two bedrooms beyond the empty sitting area, and coming to the first one, she opened the door.

There in the bed, unmoving, lay old Mrs. McGregor. Curled on her side facing the door with her arm outstretched, Jane could tell she was not breathing, but she had to be sure. Creeping towards her still form, Jane forced herself to inspect the woman. With a shaking hand, she managed to feel the woman's wrist. Finding her cold and stiff, Jane knew she was beyond help and had passed some time ago.

Unable to react as she would wish, Jane turned and left the room, shutting the door firmly behind her. She knew she had heard crying, so there was someone she could help, even if she was too late to help old Mrs. McGregor. Walking down the short hall and into the other room, Jane somehow found the courage to push open the door that had stood ajar.

This room was bigger, with a large bed in the corner and a small pallet near the door. It was on the pallet that she found the source of the crying. The McGregors had three children: a six-month-old baby girl, a three-year-old boy, and a seven-year-old girl. The older two children were huddled together on the pallet, their eyes wide at her presence. Kneeling down, Jane checked them over. Both seemed unwell, with a disheveled and pallid appearance.

She struggled for a moment, trying to remember their names before saying, "Hello, Grace and Allen. Do you remember me? My name is Jane, and I have come to check on you. How are you feeling?" Grace patted her little brother on the shoulder in a reassuring fashion that cast Jane's mind back to her own childhood when she and Elizabeth would try their best, even as children, to protect their younger siblings.

"I have been trying to care for 'im, miss. But thers no more bread, an' I ain't strong enough to draw more water." Tears welled up in Grace's worried brown eyes before trailing tracks down her grimy cheeks.

Allen did not speak, but only stared. It seemed that he was either too sick to speak or too overwhelmed. Jane felt it was probably the latter. Glancing to the bed where Allen had trained his gaze, her eyes widened before she forced herself to turn back and smile at them both. Reaching out, she ruffled Allen's hair before speaking to Grace. "You have done a remarkable job thus far do you mind if I try to help?"

"Please." Grace bit her lip before glancing at the bed and back at Jane.

"Why don't I check on your parents?" Bolstering her courage, Jane stood and walked over to the bed.

The sight that greeted her struck her like a blow. In the bed lay the three remaining McGregors. It was obvious to her, even without checking, that Mr. McGregor was dead. Several flies were flying around his boated and discolored face. He might have passed before even his mother and was most likely the source of the horrid smell the permeated the room. Forcing herself to move closer, Jane was startled to realize that Mrs. Mercy McGregor was still breathing, albeit in a shallow, raspy way. The sound of her labored breaths was more akin to a gurgled rattle than healthy breathing. Tapping her lightly, she tried to get her to respond. Calling her name did nothing, nor did shaking her. Jane wondered idly how long she had been lying in her bed next to her dead husband.

Swallowing hard, Jane leaned over and unwrapped the small bundle in Mercy's arms to check on baby Patience. It only took a glance before Jane covered the poor thing back up. Looking back at the two frightened children, Jane was all at once overcome by the enormity of the situation. Offering a warm smile, Jane said, "I am just going to go outside and draw some water. Wait right here. I will be back soon."

Dashing from the room and the house, Jane barely made it across the yard before she started vomiting.

BINGLEY KNEW THAT HIS horse was not nearly as splendid as some of Darcy's carefully bred stock, but he still loved his mare. Her Gaelic name, Nola, was a nod to the large patch of white on her shoulder amongst her otherwise brown coat. She had been one of the last things his father had given him. In fact, the horse had arrived just after the funeral.

He had taken a ride that morning, eager to get some exercise and get away from everyone for a while. Despite being a normally jovial people person, he still liked taking time by himself on occasion. This morning, he wanted to think about the last several weeks he had spent at Pemberley.

He had tried very hard to give Jane space, allowing her to move at her own speed. Jane seemed more than happy to spend time with him, and they had several very encouraging conversations. There was much they agreed on. With every day that passed, he was more convinced that she was not only the woman of his heart but would be an amazing helpmate. At times, he thought that things were progressing well, but other times, he wondered if he should have been going about things in a different manner.

He knew from conversations with the various Bennets that though she had been very popular during the season, she had left London unhappy by the experience. On the one hand, he was disturbed that she had come away from her experience in London disillusioned. On the other hand, he was happy that he still had the opportunity to prove himself to her.

It did not take him long to realize part of his issue. He knew Jane well enough to realize that she was everything that was proper. She would never approach him about her feelings. She may very well feel strongly about him and would not approach him, which meant that he would need to act. The very thought was terrifying.

The possibility of rejection loomed over him like a dark cloud, threatening to crush his spirit and leave him feeling defeated. Would things become awkward? Darcy was his closet friend, and he spent a lot of his time in his company. He wanted her happiness, but what would he do if her happiness put her in the arms of another man?

How would he handle it if he had to watch Jane fall in love with someone else? Could he see her with another man and not become desolate? He did not think so. So where did that leave him? In a horrible limbo, afraid to act, because at least at the moment, he had the hope of her love.

Stopping at the top of a hill, Bingley took in the expansive view. There were cottages and fields dotting the landscape. He had been working with Darcy to understand the way estates were managed. The fields would soon be full of workers sowing crops, and the cycle of planting and harvesting would continue.

Bingley knew that nearly everything he could see from his vantage point was Darcy's land. It wasn't for nothing that people said he owned half of Derbyshire. Bingley knew that any estate he purchased would never be nearly as sizable, but he already knew it would not deter Jane should she truly love him.

Sudden movement at the little cottage at the base of the slight rise had him swinging his horse around to investigate. Looking closely, Bingley was shocked to see Jane in the yard outside the cottage, her hands on her knees, leaning over. Without conscious thought, Bingley was urging his horse to rush to her side. Something was obviously wrong; he could see it in every line of her body, even from this distance.

HOT BILE RUSHED UP her throat, burning as it fought its way free of her stomach, and all Jane could do was lose herself in retching. She was quickly free of her breakfast, but the horror of it all and her visceral reaction did not allow her a moment's relief. It went on forever; it seemed. Eventually, all she could do was dry heave and moan plaintively. Her every muscle trembled in protest at their misuse, and Jane worried that she would soon collapse.

Then an arm was there, wrapping its way around her middle, lending her support. Jane wanted to look and see who had come to her aid but found she could not but limply rest in their arms.

"I have you, my love, I have you. I am here," Mr. Bingley's voice crooned. Eventually, when it seemed that she had finally finished, Mr. Bingley scooped her up, and carried her over to the shade. Then, sitting down, he said, "Catch your breath and then you can tell me how I can help." Mr. Bingley gently passed her a handkerchief, understanding her need to wipe her mouth before enfolding her in a warm embrace.

Not caring about propriety at the moment, Jane leaned into him and simply breathed in his clean scent, only realizing in that moment how badly the McGregors house had smelled of death. Jane counted ten deep breaths and then another ten more before she felt settled enough to speak. "They are dead, Charles. Mr. McGregor, his mother, and little baby Patience, all dead. Mrs. McGregor lives, but only barely, and I suspect that she is very close to dying." Jane paused, a catch in her throat preventing the truth from passing her lips.

Swallowing convulsively, she forced herself to say, "She still clutches her dead baby to her chest, as if love alone could save her."

Bingley clutched her to him in a way that almost seemed reflexive, tightening his arms around her in response to her horrible words. With a gasp, Charles muttered under his breath, and Jane chose not to react to his shocked words. If she was another woman, she might have been saying a few choice words as well.

After a moment, Charles composed himself and said, "Darcy will be crushed. He knows all these families. Sometimes their families have been tenants on Pemberley land for generations."

"It was much the same at Longbourn before my father brought it all teetering down." Leaning her forehead against Charles's chest, Jane attempted to draw some of his strength into her veins. He was not merely Mr. Bingley, not anymore. Somehow, in the moment he held her, their relationship stopped being so formal, and instead became what it was destined to become. Sighing, she leaned back and said, "I have to get up. There is much to do and decisions that must be made. There are two terrified children in there and a woman who might very well be taking her last breath."

Standing up, Charles helped her to her feet as well. "How can I help? What needs to be done?"

"William needs to know what is going on. I think this may very well be the beginning of an epidemic. Every family I visited this morning has been sick, though not nearly this bad." Jane walked a few steps and then turned back to Charles. "We must do what we can to prevent the spread of this illness. If at all possible, we need to keep it away from Pemberley. Elizabeth cannot for any reason try to come to help. I suspect she is with child, and despite how healthy she is, if she catches whatever this is, she could lose the baby."

Staring hard at her, Charles asked, "Am I correct in assuming that you are going to stay here to care for them?"

Gazing back into his blue eyes that seemed to speak all on their own, Jane nodded. "Yes. I doubt that the mother has long at this point, and trying to move her will just hasten her death."

Jane watched Charles nod and then, after rolling his shoulders as if fighting some urge that he found hard to control, he responded, "I understand. I will ride to Pemberley and warn Darcy. You will need supplies and medicine at the very least. Do you need help with anything before I go?"

Jane watched Charles, knowing intrinsically that he hated the idea of her staying, but he would not oppose her. She had wondered once if he respected her, and this moment was no better example of proof in the affirmative. In that frozen moment, she was finally realizing just how perfect he was for her and how petty her fears felt against such a horrible backdrop. Locking eyes with him, Jane struggled to find the right words to express what she was feeling. Finally giving up, she simply said, "Do you know how to draw water from the well?"

BINGLEY URGED HIS MARE as fast as he safely could on his return to Pemberley. It was a good thing he was so familiar with his friend's estate as he was able to take the swiftest route without issue. Though as he went, he wished that there had been someone else to send. Simply knowing he had to leave Jane there to deal with such a catastrophe in his absence left an ache in his chest.

It was not that he doubted her ability. Without a doubt, he believed she was capable of doing whatever was necessary to look after those in her care. He had long known that Jane had the strength of tempered steel when it came down to it. The problem, for him at least, was that he yearned to share her burden. What kind of man would he be if he did not want to support the woman that he loved during her trials? A burdened shared was a burdened halved after all.

It would never do to shield her from the world, lock her away on a high shelf as some society gentlemen might. The ones who only saw her beauty and the placid smile she offered to the world at large would expect nothing from her. They would let her accomplish nothing because they had no faith in her, whereas Bingley had faith in abundance. Even if it made him ache as he rode towards Pemberley, he knew Jane would manage.

He arrived at Pemberley, a dust trail rising behind him. Pulling back on the reins, Bingley slowed to a stop as he reached the massive structure that was his friend's home. Bingley was glad to see a groom rushing to greet him. Jumping down from his horse, he called out, "Nola will need to be walked and rubbed down. We need a wagon readied to go as soon as possible, and somebody send Darcy out."

It turned out that no one needed to find Darcy as he was rushing down the steps towards him. "What is going on?"

Realizing the need to keep things quiet, Bingley looked at his friend with an unusual seriousness and said in a low voice, "Three people have died at the McGregor farm. I came upon Jane just after she found them." Gritting his teeth, Bingley could not help but recall the anguish he had witnessed on her countenance. It would have devastated her to have witnessed such a loss, and he had left her there with those poor children and their dead and dying family. He knew beyond a doubt that he could have done nothing else, but it still killed him to have done it. "Jane went to visit tenants today, and she said that every family she saw had those suffering from some kind of illness. She is afraid it might be an epidemic."

Bingley watched his friend as the news hit him. While Darcy had always had difficulty socializing with groups and talking with strangers, it did not mean he was cold or unfeeling. In fact, he felt deeply and right at that moment, Bingley could read it all on his friend's face—Darcy was devastated.

Darcy cleared his throat as if struggling to speak. "Is...is Jane still there?"

"Yes, she insisted on staying. Two of the children are well enough, but she said Mr. McGregor, his mother, and the baby have passed, and Jane does not think Mrs. McGregor will last much longer."

The lines of Darcy's face grew tight. "In that case, we will see to the bodies and bring the children here to care for them."

Shaking his head, Bingley denied his friend, "No, whatever this is, it is contagious, and I have orders to do whatever I must to keep it away from Pemberley. Jane is worried about Mrs. Darcy. She suspects

Mrs. Darcy is with child, and is afraid of what could happen if she catches the illness." Running his hand through his already messy hair, Bingley continued, "We must find a way to isolate the sick but still care for them somehow."

Eyes wide, Darcy nodded, and Bingley could see that his comment had hit home. It appeared that Jane was not the only one with suspicions. After a moment of thought, Darcy said, "I will first summon the apothecary from Meryton. Then we will need volunteers to bury the dead. I should also send word to the vicar in Kympton."

"Good plan. I had a grandmother who spoke of an epidemic that swept through her town, but for the life of me, I cannot think of what she said they did to help." As they spoke, Bingley fought the feeling of every muscle twisting up in knots. Back and shoulders tense, Bingley craved action, but he was at a loss to realize how he could fight a sickness.

"Supply lines." Neither man had realized that Mrs. Bennet had approached their conversation until she began speaking. She waited until they both got over their shock at her appearance before saying, "The people who are acting as middlemen or interacting with the sick can stay at Glenn Cottage. The family that was living there has recently left, but there are beds, and we can stock it with linens and other supplies. Jane is right—we must isolate Pemberley and separate the sick. I will see to the medical supplies that need to be taken out to the ill families."

Looking at Mrs. Bennet, Bingley asked, "Jane said she was going to take care of the McGregor children. If Mrs. McGregor dies, should Jane still care for them there? Or should the children be brought somewhere else?"

Bingley watched emotions play over Mrs. Bennet's face. In the hard line of her lips, he could see her determination, but in the softening around her eyes, he could see her compassion. After a moment, she spoke, her voice even but not unkind. "If they are ill, they should be cared for in their homes, if possible. We do not want this spreading and I do not think the other families who are already sick should be burdened with additional sick children."

"THOSE POOR CHILDREN. WE must find a way to help them through this." Elizabeth stood from her chair and began pacing the room. She continued speaking, "Jane is going to need blankets and linens. Mama will get all the tinctures and herbs, but she will need food and—"

Darcy followed his distraught wife and embraced her. "Calm down, my love. We will take care of your sister and the McGregors, but you need to stop and breathe." Darcy knew that telling Elizabeth about the spreading illness would upset her. He only hoped that she would be reasonable when he explained the plans they were putting in place to care for the ill. Somehow he knew he was about to have a fight on his hands.

Elizabeth shuddered but laid her forehead against his chest and managed to breathe deeply for a time. Even with her deep breaths, Darcy knew she was not feeling at all calm and could feel the tension in his wife as she gripped his waistcoat. Too soon, she brought her head up and looked up into his face. "I must go to her! I cannot let her deal with this alone."

It hurt Darcy to see Elizabeth emerald eye's awash in tears. He would do almost anything to take that worry and sorrow away from her expression, but there was too much at risk in that moment. "Actually, your sister told Bingley that you were not to be allowed anywhere near any of the sick tenants or their homes." As soon as the words left his mouth, Darcy braced himself.

"What?" Elizabeth screeched. Jerking back from Darcy, she glared up at him, fury in her gaze. "You did not just say that I was to be kept from my sister." Moving several steps away from Darcy, Elizabeth's anger sizzled in the air, though she never once averted her gaze.

Locking eyes with Elizabeth, Darcy refused to flinch. Instead, he said, "Jane is insistent that you do not go to help her, and your mother supports her decision."

Elizabeth resumed pacing around the room. Her voice was sharp, with no effort to hide her feelings, as she said, "That is ridiculous. Jane and Mother are simply being silly. I am healthy. Even if I come down with whatever this is, I doubt I would be worse for it." Looking over her shoulder at Darcy, Elizabeth bit out, "I would never stay away from one of my sisters when she needed me. Nothing has ever stopped me from helping Jane before. Nothing will stop me now."

Elizabeth's steps were punctuating her words, stomping out her frustration, and Darcy felt for her but was unmoving in his opinion that Elizabeth must be kept away from the sickness. Though it was not how he imagined having the conversation, Darcy knew the one thing that might help Elizabeth choose the wiser course. So, he used his trump card. "Not even if you are with child?"

Elizabeth's foot froze for a moment before coming down with a clatter. Swiveling around, Elizabeth faced her husband. Her mouth gaping open in shock, hanging wordlessly for a moment before saying, "With child?"

Darcy thought it was incredible to watch the emotions flitter across Elizabeth's face. The anger bled away and was overtaken by confusion and wonder. His wife was so very expressive, even without speaking. "Yes, apparently both your mother and Jane think you are pregnant and want you to stay clear of the sickness because of it."

"I... Oh my..." Elizabeth slowly made her way over to the settee she had been sitting on when Darcy had made his way into the room. She pressed one hand to her lips and the other to her stomach.

Following her to the settee, Darcy set next to her, saying quietly, "You have been tired lately. This could explain that."

"Yes, that is true. I have been more tired than I am used to, but I never thought..." Once again, Elizabeth drifted off mid-sentence.

Darcy's lips twitched as he took in his wife's turmoil. She was such a dynamic woman. It was not often that he got to see her so overwhelmed. "It's not as if it's impossible," Darcy said.

Closing her eyes, Elizabeth seemed to be pondering something before she rested her second hand at her waist along with the first. "No, it is more than possible. Though I had not thought that a baby could be the reason I was tired, but Mama and Jane know what they are about." Looking at Darcy, Elizabeth smiled. "There is no way to be certain until I feel the babe move, and that will be months from now."

Finding it impossible not to smile at the news, Darcy said, "Until then, I want to keep you and the little one safe." Darcy held his hand out to her, wanting to soothe away her upset. "Everyone wants that."

Elizabeth took his hand in her own and squeezed it tight. She tried to smile, but it came out wobbly as she whispered, "I hate not being there for Jane. I have always managed to protect my family, to be there for them. This feels as though I am failing here somehow."

Taking her hand, he pulled it up to kiss her knuckles, maintaining eye contact as he did so. Then, placing her hand over his heart, he said, "Can you not see this as protecting your family? A newer member of your family? Jane would never begrudge you that. Remember, she is the one who told us to keep you away. I am sure you can find another way to be helpful."

"You are right. I would never do anything to risk a gift as precious as what we may have been granted." Sighing, Elizabeth leaned into Darcy, and he wrapped his arms around her form. They sat there in silence for a moment before she said, "What do you think you will want to be called?"

Smiling into his wife's hair, Darcy said, "I think Papa will suit me very well."

IN THE END, IT did not take long for Bingley to be on his way back to the McGregors on a fresh horse. He was accompanied by a wagon with several strong men who had volunteered to help with the interring of the dead and shuttling supplies. A kitchen maid named Susan had also come along to help Jane care for the sick, whether at the McGregors' or elsewhere.

Susan had told him, "My grandma was often called to help the sick, and it was many a time that I went with her. Besides, someone will need to do the cooking and cleaning while Miss Bennet cares for the ill." Though Bingley had never met the young woman before, he was impressed with her attitude and bravery.

Looking over the stocked wagon, Bingley was glad that they had as many supplies as they did. There was food and medicine in the wagon, as well as a trunk that Mrs. Bennet had sent for Jane. Bingley had brought his own supplies, having easily decided that he would not be returning to stay at Pemberley until matters had resolved. He would stay at Glenn Cottage, and he would help in the field, so to say. Darcy had wanted to come, but Bingley had managed to convince him to stay at Pemberley to oversee things.

Chapter Eight

Jane looked up from her task at the sound of a wagon approaching. Smiling down at Grace and Allen, she said, "I hear a wagon. It seems we will have some visitors."

She had been using a wet rag to clean up both children as best she could. Allen seemed to be suffering from a fever, and she hoped it would cool him. Grace, on the other hand, was not sick as far as Jane could tell. They seemed to settle under her kind attention. Both had been very grateful to have the water that she had offered for them to drink. Mrs. McGregor had not regained consciousness, but Jane had wet the woman's lips. Jane feared that trying to even drip some water into her mouth might worsen her condition if she choked.

Getting up from where she knelt on the floor next to the children's pallet, Jane murmured, "I am going to greet our guests. They will probably come inside. I do not want you to be frightened by the strangers; they are here to help." Grace nodded in response to Jane's statement, wrapping her arm around her little brother. Allen did respond but continued staring, his wide brown eyes nearly unblinking. Jane ruffled Grace's hair and smiled at her encouragingly. "You are such a brave little girl and a wonderful big sister."

Moments later, Jane was in the yard, greeting the people who had arrived. She nearly fell back against the doorjamb when she spotted Charles, her relief was so great. She wished she could have taken a moment to analyze her reaction and her desire to call him by his Christian name, but there would not be time for such musings about her heart until the calamity had been thoroughly handled.

Charles jumped down from his horse and jogged closer, saying, "I have brought help and supplies. How are you bearing up?"

Jane grimaced, looking over at the others coming down from the wagon. Turning back to Charles, she said, "I will be much better once the bodies have been removed and we can give everything a thorough cleaning."

The older of the two men came over, and Jane vaguely recognized him as someone who worked in the stables. Removing his cap, he crushed it in his large, calloused hands. Clearing his throat, he said, "James and I will get to work digging some graves. Mr. Darcy said that we should bury them as swiftly as we can to keep this from spreading."

"Thank you for being willing to help at a time like this, Mr....?"

"Greg Eliot, ma'am." Rubbing at a spot of dirt on his pants, the large man shook his head. "It is no trial, miss. If a beautiful lady such as yourself is willing to help succor the sick and dying, I can do no less." Nodding to her, he and the second man, James, turned towards the back of the wagon and retrieved the shovels. They set off, diligently searching for a spot where the small family could be laid to rest.

After they left, a young woman of about Kitty's age came forward and bobbed a curtsy. "My name's Susan, Miss Bennet." The girl offered an explanation, seemingly aware of Jane's lack of recognition. "I work down in the kitchens, miss. I have come to help you with the cooking and cleaning and caring for the sick ones. I have some bit of training from my grandmother. Not a lot, mind you, but I am a hard worker. I will do right by you."

Stepping forward, Jane grasped the girl's hand in a move that seemed to have been unexpected if Susan's expression meant anything. "Thank you so much for being willing to help. I think we may very well have our work cut out for us."

A quick blush flashed across Susan's cheeks, but she managed to respond, "Thank you, miss. I will just go inside and see about starting in the kitchen."

Jane watched the girl go into the house, glad to have help about the place. As much as Jane was accustomed to working in the stillroom or in the garden, she hadn't the first idea about how she would have put that kitchen in order.

It was unsettling to Jane that she still did not know all the workers and servants at Pemberley. She had lived there off and on for months, but it was not like Longbourn. Whereas Longbourn had no more than ten servants, Pemberley had five or six times that.

Going back to Charles, she smiled wanly at him. "You cannot know how relieved I am to have you back."

"And you do not know how glad I am to have been able to return to you." Charles took her hand and squeezed it. "Is there anything I could do that would be helpful?"

Tilting her head, Jane sighed. "It has occurred to me that this might not be the only family so affected. There could be any number of families that are as bad off as the McGregors. Once we have a few things settled here, would you mind riding out to all the tenant homes and checking on them? We need to know how many people are sick and where they are."

Eyes squinting in the bright of the day, Charles seemed to ponder the problem before nodding his head. "That is something I can easily see to. It might take a few days to check on all the families with as many of them as there are, but it can be done." Gazing over to the little clearing where the two men were digging graves, and then at the wagon full of supplies, he returned his attention to Jane. "The four of us have no plans to return to Pemberley until this is all over. Your mother suggested that there is an unused building where we gentlemen can stay at in order to quarantine and prevent the spread as much as possible. Meanwhile, you and Susan will stay here."

"Thank you." Jane saw the risk of what they were all doing and could only be grateful that she was not in the struggle alone. "I should go inside and check on the children. I think I will need to have a conversation with them about us burying their father, sister, and grandmother. It would be best to move the bodies out of the home as soon as we can, but I am uncertain they even realize that they have died."

Charles's eyes bore into Jane's and somehow, she knew he could comprehend the pain she had felt. How many men would see that at a time like this? After a pregnant pause full of silent conversation and compassion, he said, "Let me know if I can help tell them. I would like to meet them both, but I will let you decide when that will be best."

"I think that would be good, though I am uncertain when the best time will be. I really should get back to them and see about helping to prepare everything for taking the bodies away for burial." Jane froze, a look of heartache crossing her face. The young family that had been so happy with the birth of young Patience not six months ago would never be the same. In all likelihood, those children would be orphans in the span of a few hours, and she was forced to worry about the logistics of getting the deceased bodies buried. The weight of confronting the harsh realities of life felt unbearable. Closing her eyes, she concentrated on breathing through her sorrow. She had tasks she had to accomplish; she could not wallow in sadness.

Then she felt Charles's hand on her shoulder and his whisper in her ear. "You are not alone in this. Whatever needs doing, we will do it together."

Jane found her lips wobbling as she tried to smile. Her usual mask of calm acceptance faltered, but as she looked up into Charles's eyes, she wondered if it wasn't as much of a problem as she thought. He did not seem to mind her wet eyes and broken smile. Swallowing thickly, she said, "Thank you. You do not know how much your support means to me."

Giving her shoulder a squeeze, Charles said, "You go inside and see to the children. I will start unloading the wagon."

After watching him turn away and get to work, Jane moved into the building, blinking to allow her eyes to adjust to the darker setting. It was easy to spot Susan bustling around, and Jane found herself smiling at Susan's industrious movements. She scuttled about the room, gathering all the dirty cups, plates, and pans in sight before placing them all in a large tub. Noting Jane's presence, Susan nervously offered an explanation. "It is quite the mess in here, but I had assumed as much when I volunteered. Once I get all this gathered, I will start the stove and get some hot water going for washing and the like."

"I am sure you have it all in hand. Do tell me if you need assistance with anything. I am going to look in on the children and Mrs. McGregor."

Returning to the dark back room where the children waited for her, Jane could not help but wrinkle her nose at the stench. She could only hope that as soon as they had the kitchen in hand and the bodies buried, they could start cleaning and washing laundry. It was not the family's fault that things had progressed to such a state, but that did not make her long for strong soap and hot water any less.

The children had barely moved an inch in her absence. At least Allen had finally stopped staring at his unmoving parents. Grace was using the rag that Jane had left to cool little Allen's brow.

Smiling, she knelt next to the two. "Grace, you are such a good sister. Has he fallen asleep?"

"Yes, I think so." Grace's voice was small and trembled slightly as she spoke. "I thought Papa was asleep at first, too." Little lip trembling, Grace gazed at Jane, her eyes too full of knowledge for a child of her years.

"Do not worry, Grace, your brother is just sleeping. Look, you can tell. Watch his chest rise and fall." Jane directed Grace's gaze to her brother's sleeping form, his chest rising and falling with little puffing breaths. They sat for a moment in the near silence, simply watching the boy breathe, before Jane finally forced herself to say what she must. "You are right, though; your Papa is not sleeping. He and your grandmother and little baby Patience were too sick, and they died."

Biting her lip, Grace asked, "What about Mama? Is she going to die too?"

"Your mother is very sick. It is very possible that she may die, but then again, she may not. I cannot say what is going to happen." Jane watched Grace carefully, worried about her solemn acceptance. Grace had little to no reaction. She merely looked down and then continued to pat her brother's forehead with the damp rag.

Eventually, Grace whispered, "Mama said I had to be brave and take care of Allen."

Understanding made Jane shudder at the memories that resurfaced. She could well remember pushing her own anxieties away to take care of her younger siblings and soothe their fears and worries. It was probably one of the reasons she had come to rely on her smile so much. Jane struggled with the lump in her throat before she could say, "Soon some men are coming in here to take your papa, grandma, and little sister away to bury them. It is not healthy to keep them here."

Focused on her brother, Grace diligently cleansed his face, her words filled with a mix of sadness and acceptance. "At least they will be together."

In the end, it was a simple affair to remove the three McGregors and inter them into the simple graves. They used the blankets from their beds to wrap them, as they had no coffins. Jane knew she would never forget the sight of those bundles being taken away. She chose not to see them buried; she stayed with the children instead. Was it a coward's action to not want to see them slowly covered with dirt? Or did she truly feel the need to stay with the children as they mourned the loss of all they knew?

BINGLEY MADE HIS WAY into the sickroom as quietly as he could manage. Jane was busy with Susan scrubbing out the other room. He wanted to check in on the children while Jane and Susan were occupied. He did not want to disturb Mrs. McGregor or the children if they were sleeping. At first glance, Mrs. McGregor appeared unchanged based on Jane's description of the woman. She was still unconscious, rasping with every breath. He watched her for only a moment before turning away. He knew there was nothing he could do for her, and it hurt to acknowledge that to himself.

So he focused on the children. He liked children, though he rarely spent any time with them. None of his friends had children and his sister Louisa had only recently had her baby. He was looking forward to the time when he would be able to play with the lad. For now, though, he was happy enough to be to be working on his relationship with Jane.

Right away, he noticed that the little girl was silently watching him, so Bingley smiled and asked, "Would you mind if I sit down?"

After a moment's hesitation, Grace smiled tentatively and nodded her head. Approaching slowly, he sat down cross-legged, all the while maintaining his smile. He did not want to scare the children on top of everything else. Figuring introductions were in order, he said, "My name is Charles Bingley."

Grace responded by saying, "My name is Grace McGregor, and this is my little brother Allen."

Hearing his name, little Allen rolled over and rubbed at his eyes, mumbling, "Wha?"

Grace, showing ample mothering instincts, patted her brother on the shoulder reassuringly. "Do not worry, Allen. I was just introducing you to Mr. Bingley."

Trying to bring as much normalcy to the situation as possible, Bingley said, "It is nice to meet you, Grace, and you as well, Allen. Though if you want, you can call me Charles." He watched the two siblings and wondered how the tragedy they were experiencing would affect them throughout their lives.

Sitting up, Allen looked around and asked, "Where is Miss Jane?"

"She is eating, but I told her I would come in and spend time with you so you would not be lonely," Bingley explained, eager to reassure the boy. Spotting a pitcher of water and a pair of cups, he asked, "Are either of you thirsty? Would you like some water?"

Allen nodded his head. "Yes, please, Mr. Charles."

Reaching over, Bingley's long reach allowed him to grab the pitcher and cups without having to get up from his spot. Filling both cups with a small amount of water, he handed them to Allen and Grace, respectively. He watched Allen gulp his down and said, "Be careful you do not choke. I can always get you more."

As Allen slowed his water consumption to a more sedate pace, Grace, unlike her brother, sipped at her water slowly. Eventually Allen stopped drinking and just looked at his cup, until suddenly he blurted out, "My papa died, an' Grandma and baby Pa'tince." The comment might have seemed random, but Bingley was unruffled. It was one of the reasons he liked children. They said what was on their mind.

"I am sorry about that, Allen. I know how sad you must be. Both of my parents and my older brother died, too."

AFTER THE BURIAL, CHARLES took the time to console the children before seeking Jane out. He informed her of his plan to visit the families living nearby and then bring supplies to Glenn Cottage, where the men would be staying for the duration of the epidemic.

She watched him mount his horse and ride away, vaguely marveling at how attached she had become to him. She had known she had feelings for him for some time, but the desire to keep him with her was a surprising development. Squaring her shoulders, Jane turned back to the house to face the task of seeing to the living.

Jane was extremely grateful that her mother, or possibly Elizabeth, had sent so many clean linens. It enabled Susan and her to make a pallet on the floor where they could place Mrs. McGregor while they remade the bed, used the quilt to wrap her husband and baby, and removed the soiled sheets for washing.

After giving the unconscious woman a sponge bath, they resettled her in her bed and Jane was at least confident that she was resting more comfortably. Wiping her sweaty brow with her forearm, Jane left the bedroom and went in search of Susan, who had bundled up all the soiled linens and took them away. Finding her at the stove heating a large pot of water, Jane asked, "How are you holding up?"

"Well enough, miss. I am hoping some of the hardest work is behind us, though all of this laundry will be a task in itself." Gesturing with her chin toward the container of lye soap on the table, Susan said, "At least we have plenty of good, strong soap. I can start on the mopping and cleaning the various rooms once I have the laundry started."

Jane nodded in agreement before saying, "Thank you for all of your hard work, Susan. You are doing a marvelous job. I was just thinking we should try to ensure cleanliness in hopes of not getting sick ourselves. I plan to place a bowl of water and a small pot of soft soap outside the family's room, allowing everyone to wash their hands whenever they exit." Rolling her head back and forth to loosen some of her tense muscles, she added, "I also had an idea that you and I could stay in the smaller bedroom tonight once we have finished cleaning it."

Turning her back to the stove, Susan nodded her head, her expression contemplative. "I think that is a good idea. I have opened the windows around the house. Hopefully we can air it out some and clear out the smell."

"Yes, that will clear the air, and I also have an idea that may help." Jane thought back to the old book she had found of her grandmother's full of advice to the future generations. If only there had been something in there about dealing with the sorrow that came with helping the sick. Swallowing around the lump in her throat, Jane said, "My grandmother had a recipe that she claimed would help clear out sickness in the air. I do not know if it will help, but it cannot hurt."

Nodding, Susan asked, "How are the children?"

Jane shook her head. "Quiet, especially little Allen. I cannot imagine what they have gone through or what is going through their minds. Allen's fever is not as bad as it could be. I am hoping that we can keep him drinking enough tea and broth to help him fight it off."

"What about little Gracie?"

"She does not seem to be sick yet, but I would not be surprised if she comes down with it. She has been so exposed; I do not know how she could escape it."

GRACE LOOKED DOWN AT her brother as he mumbled in his sleep. It was something he often did, and if she was not so worried, she would have smiled. Smoothing the sweaty hair from her brother's forehead, Grace forced her gaze to where her mother lay in bed. She tried to tell herself that she was not frightened by the rattling sound that came from her mother, but she knew that sound could not be good. Miss Jane had not looked hopeful when she was helping Mama.

For now, Grace was alone with her sick brother and Mama because the nice lady had gone out into the kitchen. Grace had been so worried when they ran out of water and bread. Now, with Miss Jane arriving and the other people, there would be food and water and clean blankets. It was better food than the stale bread she had been trying to get her brother to eat. Miss Jane had already brought them tea with honey to drink, along with a bowl of broth for both her and her brother. It had tasted better than anything Grace could remember.

Leaning her head against the wall behind her, Grace sighed, tears tracking their way down her cheeks. Her head ached, but she was too focused on her brother to tell Miss Jane about it. She felt better than either her brother or her mama; she did not need help as much as they did. Gazing back at her mama from the pallet where she sat with her brother, Grace watched her chest rise and fall. She had been asleep for a long time, days even. Grace was starting to worry that just like Grandma and Papa, she was not going to wake up.

THE SMELL OF CLOVE, cinnamon, and rosemary was an odd combination, but it did indeed help clear the air of the smell of decay and loss. Jane knew her grandmother's recipe also called for lemon and orange peel, but they did not have any on hand at the moment. Even without the scent of citrus added to the mix, Jane was happy with the result. Who would have thought simmering herbs and spices in a pot with water could make such a difference? Now they just needed to keep adding water occasionally to keep the fragrant steam going.

It was endearing to watch how much Grace, a child herself, wanted to care for her younger brother. Jane wondered if it had anything to do with all the loss that she had experienced or if it was an oldest daughter trait. She had lost three family members in swift succession and would most likely lose her mother soon. It was understandable that she would cling to who she had left.

Kneeling on the floor, Jane asked, "How is Allen, Grace?"

Grace smiled wanly, her hands constantly fussing about her brother. Smoothing his hair before looking up at Jane, she said, "His fever is not that bad, but he is sleeping."

"That's good; rest is good for you when you are unwell." Jane smiled at the boy. His flushed cheeks and sweaty brow told her he was still ill. She was overly concerned, as he was breathing naturally and woke easily when she brought tea and broth. Looking at Grace's tired face, she asked, "Would you like more tea or a bite to eat?"

Grace shook her head, her lank hair flying about before saying, "No, I am still full."

Jane nodded; she did not want to overtax the girl's system. She paused before saying, "Actually, I was thinking you could probably use a nap as well."

Pressing her lips together, Grace shook her head in denial. Eventually, she said, "I should be caring for Allen. I can sleep later." Her voice was soft, her gaze almost desperate.

Jane reached out to smooth the hair back from the young girl's face. The poor thing was drooping with exhaustion, but still she struggled on. Jane knew the feeling of having the world rest on your shoulders. The ache of fearing not for yourself but for your family. "I know you want to care for your brother, but I am here now. I will look after Allen, and we can both care for him after you rest." Jane helped rearrange Grace from a sitting position so that she could lie down next to her brother, encouraging her to relax. Watching the girl's eyes droop, Jane rubbed a line soothingly back and forth along her forehead, hoping to lull her to sleep. Jane waited until the child finally slept before leaning back on her heels. She paused a moment to make sure both children were sound asleep before leaving their sides.

Getting up off the floor, Jane moved to sit on the chair by the bed. While both children were sleeping, she felt compelled to spend time with Mercy McGregor before she went back to help Susan. Sadly,

Jane knew Mercy was not long for the world. It would most likely not be too long before she passed away. Jane could hear a rasping rattle come with Mercy's every breath. Jane had cared for dying people in the past and had heard that sound before; it was never a good sign.

It was frustrating to know that she did not have the ability to save the woman and could only make her comfortable. Her fever was not high, but Jane knew she was slipping away, and she simply did not have the means to fight a sickness that had progressed so far. With Mercy unconscious, she could not get her to drink any of the tinctures or teas that she possessed. It had settled deep into her lungs and would be the death of her. Leaning over, Jane smoothed Mercy's hair, humming a lullaby under her breath. She had no idea if Mercy was aware of anything at this point, but she could not begrudge her some comfort. It did not hurt that Jane was comforted by the lullaby herself.

THE STRESS IN THE house had driven Lydia out of doors and into the refuge of her flowers. What did it matter if she was weeding a little more vigorously than necessary? It was a relief to take her frustrations out on the plants that wanted to choke the life out of her babies.

There was so little that Lydia could do to help the situation. Jane was off helping the poor orphans and putting herself at risk while she nursed them back to health. Despite getting extra sleep, Elizabeth was always tired, but it did not stop her from keeping Pemberley running smoothly and making sure everyone was hale and hardy. Mother had taken charge of various things, ensuring that the afflicted families had their needs tended to. Mary and Georgianna had started making clothes and toys for the two children who had so much of their world taken away by cruel fate. Kitty, never one to cope well with difficulties, had started painting and had not seemed to stop.

That left Lydia to her own rather frustrated devices. Though she wished she could go help Jane, she knew it was not something she could do. Everyone was too afraid of contagion to take risks. It seemed that the situation was under control and being well managed by Mr. Bingley and Jane, but that did not soothe Lydia. She was still outside, stabbing at uncooperative weeds that were trying to steal nutrients from her roses.

"What did that plant ever do to you?" Kiernan's voice had Lydia's head coming up from its determined pursuit in search of her young friend.

Finding him behind her, Lydia grinned, saying, "Nothing really, but it is satisfying to stab at something sometimes and weeds should not be here trying to take over the rose bed."

"I can see how that could be fun. Do you need some help?" Kiernan said, rolling up his sleeves and preparing to assist her.

Tilting her head, Lydia pondered for a moment before asking, "I thought you had time with your tutor today. Are you avoiding your lessons for some reason?"

"Nah." Kiernan shook his head with a mischievous grin that Lydia had always been fond of. He was like the little brother she had secretly always wanted. At eleven, he was only four years younger than her fifteen-year-old self, and they had a good relationship. While he had always been especially close to Elizabeth, Kiernan viewed all the Bennet girls as his sisters. "Because of the illness, my tutor has stayed away."

Lydia picked up an extra trowel and held it aloft for him. Happy to have company, she said, "Well, as long as you do not think your mother will miss you, I would be more than happy to have you help me with weeding."

Taking the instrument, Kiernan sat down on the ground next to her. "Just tell me what we are killing. I would hate to execute the wrong plant."

Laughing, Lydia explained exactly what she had been doing and what to look out for. They worked in companionable silence for a time before Kiernan asked, "Are you worried about Miss Jane?"

Coming up short with a weed in her hands, Lydia focused on Kiernan. His brown eyes were sharp and discerning, though his flicker of a smile let Lydia know he knew he had startled her. He was often more perceptive than people gave him credit for. Between that and his sharp intelligence and thirst for learning, it was no wonder that William had arranged for him to receive tutoring and would eventually send him to Eton.

Sighing, Lydia reminded herself that she could not rub at her face without getting covered in dirt. Looking at Kiernan, she said, "Yes, I am. Jane is not one to look after herself when there are people to care for. I am afraid that she will overwork herself and then catch whatever has killed off half of the McGregors."

"Miss Jane would be just the type to do that." Kiernan paused and fiddled with the dirt, stabbing it with his trowel. Then, looking Lydia straight in the eye, he said, "You are forgetting, though, that she is not alone. Susan, the kitchen maid, went to help her. Mr. Bingley is also out there helping your sister, and I do not believe that he would allow her to put herself in jeopardy. He loves her too much."

Dropping onto her heels, her mind turned over the information that Kiernan had provided and she felt her face stretching in a wide smile. "You are right. He is rather in love with her, isn't he?"

"He is far and away lost to her."

"If only she could see how perfect he is for her." Lydia leaned forward, about to pull at another weed when she froze in place. Then, looking back at Kiernan, she laughingly said, "Do you suppose this whole situation will knock some sense into her?"

Nodding his head, Kiernan moved around to the other side of the square flower bed to work on another section of weeds. "I would not be surprised if they were engaged by the time the quarantine is over."

Returning to the work at hand, Lydia said, "I will hope for the best. Jane is more stubborn than people give her credit for. It is her smile, I think. Where Elizabeth will glare and frown, Jane smiles and keeps her mask in place, all the while not moving an inch. I'm worried that her own insecurities will hinder her from recognizing the love she has at her fingertips."

They had almost finished the bed when Kiernan spoke again. "I would not have thought it would be more difficult to get Miss Jane with Mr. Bingley than it was for Miss Elizabeth and Mr. Darcy. Not with the way he kept blundering!" This had them both bursting into tears of laughter at all their memories of how often William had ended up with his boot in his mouth.

Chapter Nine

BINGLEY ACHED IN EVERY way possible. He was not used to staying in the saddle for such an extended period of time, but it had been necessary. After leaving the McGregor cottage, Bingley rode across Pemberley lands, checking on the various families. As he rode, Bingley finally realized the true size of Darcy's property. No wonder Darcy had been so stressed when he had to take over the running of the estate after his father's death.

Some families he spoke with were perfectly fine, though many had at least one member of their family ill. None of the families had been as hard hit as the McGregors. There were no additional deaths, and it appeared that no one else was gravely ill. It was a good thing, he supposed, but that did not stop the sorrow he felt knowing how much that one family had been affected. Though his body was sore from riding, it was his heart that ached the most.

In all reality, he worried more for Jane than he did anyone else. The other men had gone to the cottage to quarantine, but Bingley needed to check on Jane. He was worried not only about her health, but about her heart. Jane was at the core soft and compassionate, and she cared deeply about people. Jane wanted everyone to be happy and healthy and often became invested in helping others. It would be heart-wrenching for her to stay and care for the sick and dying.

It had grown dark while he was at the last house, but a full moon lit his way. As he approached his destination, Bingley could see the lights shining from the windows. If he did not know what was going on in the house, he would have said the home seemed to have a hopeful look about it, shining there in the dark. Coming down off the horse, he left it to graze before going inside. He knew he would only be able to stay a short time before going back to Glenn Cottage for the night.

Susan stood at the stove, but looked up to greet Bingley when he knocked at the door and came in. Keeping his voice low, Bingley said, "Hello Susan, how are you doing this evening?"

"Oh, hello, Mr. Bingley. I am well enough." Gesturing to the kettle on the stove, she asked, "Would you like a cup of tea?"

"Not at the moment, but perhaps before I leave. I want to check on Miss Bennet and the others first. How are they doing?"

Glancing in the direction of the sickroom, Susan sighed. "The children are managing, I suppose. Young Allen is not getting any worse, but I know Miss Bennet is afraid that Grace is falling ill. Mrs. Mercy, however, I do not think will last the night."

Nodding, Bingley made his way to the sickroom and, after knocking softly, made his way in. He let his gaze slide around the room. Two children were asleep on a pallet on the floor. They did not appear healthy, but neither did they seem deathly ill. It did not take that long for Bingley to realize why Susan seemed to be so certain that Mrs. McGregor was not long for the world. Every breath she took was a gurgling struggle to draw in the air.

Jane was sitting on the bed next to the suffering woman, stroking her brow, her voice low and soothing as she said, "All is well, Mercy. Do not be afraid. I am here with you, and more importantly, God is with you. You are not alone." Bingley watched as Jane dabbed a wet cloth on Mrs. McGregor's lips. "It is all right to let go. Your children are safe and cared for. I promise that I will do everything in my power to see that they are safe and happy. They will never be alone in this world. You do not need to worry; all will be well. You may go in peace."

Bingley stood frozen, unable to move from his spot as he watched the strength of the woman he loved shine through the sadness that permeated the room. How strong did you have to be to soothe someone in such a manner? Bingley was in awe of her. His heart ached for her, and he yearned to be by her side, offering solace. However, he resisted the temptation to interrupt the profoundly poignant moment.

It was not long before Mrs. McGregor released her last breath, and the room was full of silence. Propelled forward by the sorrow that he could see on Jane's face, Bingley helped Jane to bring the blanket up over the woman's face. Bingley's mind searched for something to say to offer comfort to the woman he loved but found it impossible. He knew of no words powerful enough to provide solace at such a time.

Bingley could only stand before Jane, wondering how he could help ease some of her pain. Then, as if they were two magnets drawn by forces beyond their knowing, they both moved, and somehow Bingley was holding Jane, allowing her to sob quietly into his chest.

SOMETIMES LIFE WAS JUST too heart-wrenching to bear. Jane burrowed her face into Charles's waistcoat, trying to muffle her sobs. It was impossible for her to remain stoic and serene in that moment. Moreover, she did not want to wake the children. She did not think she could face explaining their mother's death when she had still not come to grips with it herself. Mercy had been such a smiling woman, and she had loved her children to the depth of her bones. The McGregors had been such a happy family, and now only the two children remained. How would they cope with such a traumatic loss?

Eventually, Jane realized that Charles was patting her back and crooning to her as if she were a child, and suddenly the world was not such a horrible a place. There was still light and comfort in the world and reasons to move forward despite the pain. Pulling her head back, Jane looked up into Charles's eyes. She was surprised to note that his face was painted with tears, and his eyes were red rimmed. They were a pair, matching each other in their grief.

After some time of simply staring at one another, Charles said, "Come, you need of some respite." Then, with an arm around her shoulders to hold her close, he shepherded her into the kitchen and settled her at the table. Bringing the basin over to her, he helped her wash her hands with the lye soup before washing his own. Drying their hands on a towel, he offered her his support in strength and silence.

Susan seemed to understand what had taken place with no explanation. Moving to the stove, she silently wiped away her tears. Returning, she poured the hot water into the teapot and then returned the kettle to its place on the stove. "We all need a nice calming cup of tea at times such as this."

Soon, there was a cup of tea in front of each of them as they all sat around the table, sipping in companionable silence and grief. In time, Jane looked up from watching the steam rise off her cup of tea and saw that Susan and Charles were both watching her with concern. Smiling grimly, Jane said, "I am well." She tried to smooth her hair away from her face with a sigh. When her hand encountered more of a mess than she expected, she settled for shoving her wayward hair behind her ears. "Mercy is not the first person I have tried to help who has died."

Though she had known she would not be able to save Mercy McGregor, her loss still cut like a knife. Charles's eyes sought Jane's and his tired blue gaze seemed to emphasize his words as he said, "That does not make my need to comfort you any less." Reaching out, Charles clasped her hand that lay on the table in his larger one. "What can I do to help? What do you need?"

Jane's chin wobbled for a moment before regaining her self-control. Jane knew her mask was slipping and that everyone could see her grief. It took her a moment to fight down her panic at showing weakness. She reminded herself that Charles and Susan would not judge her. Looking into Charles's gaze, she knew that he would never hurt her and, in fact, would be the first to protect her from harm. Taking a breath, Jane said, "I do not want the children to see their mother dead when they wake. Do you think it would be fitting to move her into the barn until she can be buried?"

Nodding his head, Charles said, "I am sure that would be fine."

It was horrifying to think that the children would wake to see their dead mother lying there in the morning. She could not stop the sadness they would face because of their mother's death, but she could protect them from haunting memories.

When Grace woke up, she looked around the room slowly. Based on the watery light she could see coming from under the door, she thought it was morning. She did not feel any better than the night before. In fact, she felt worse. Her throat hurt, and her head was fuzzy, but she ignored that in favor of checking on her brother.

Reaching out, she ran her fingers through her brother's hair and was happy when he said, "Stop, Gracie, I'm seeping." He then cuddled into her side, and she held him close, enjoying the warmth he brought with him.

Her relief was short-lived. As soon as she turned her head to check on her mother in the bed in the corner, Grace realized what had happened. The bed had been made up with clean sheets and a quilt she did not recognize, but it was empty. Her mother was not there. The only reason her mother would be missing was if she had died like her papa, grandma, and baby Patience. She was that much closer to being all alone.

Grace let her tears fall quietly in the dim morning light. She clung to her brother, her only remaining family, and tried to muffle her sorrow and sobs. Grace could not help but feel overwhelmed. Feeling sluggish and fuzzy made everything more difficult. There also seemed to be a great weight laying on her chest.

When the door opened quietly and Miss Jane walked into the room, their eyes met and locked. Grace saw the moment the woman noticed her tear-stained cheeks. In a rush, she came to the small pallet where Grace and Allen lay and said, "Oh, honey, I am so sorry."

Grace liked that the lady did not act as if she was too young or stupid to understand. Not every adult would act that way. "What is going to happen to us now?"

Holding her arms out, Miss Jane asked, "May I hold you? Come here, sweetheart." When Grace nodded her head, Miss Jane leaned forward and helped her to crawl into her lap. "I promised your mama that you would be taken care of. That means that I will make sure you and your brother are happy and safe. I do not know if you have any family nearby, but if you do, you might go to live with them. But

I want you to know that no matter what happens, I will make sure you are both well and are as happy as can be."

Grace closed her eyes and became lost in the comfort that Miss Jane was providing. She could almost believe it was her mother embracing her, even though she knew it wasn't. It was still nice when Miss Jane started humming and rocking her back and forth when she cried.

THE SMALL, SOFT WEIGHT of Grace's body reminded Jane of the last time she had held Lydia. Her sister had scraped her knee in a fall and had been crying, so Jane had held her until her tears had dried up. Though it was a different child she held, she hummed the same lullaby. The most obvious difference was the fact that the tears soaking into her dress were not the result of a scraped knee. The child's tears stemmed from the desolation of grief.

Jane was so glad that Charles had moved poor Mercy into the barn before he left the night before. At least Grace had not had to discover her mother's dead body when she woke. Little Grace had enough to deal with.

While Jane did not know the loss of a mother, she could imagine the sorrow Grace felt, not to mention the fear she must have for her and her brother's future. Jane wondered if Grace and Allen had any family nearby. Was there someone out there who would be willing and able to take in two children not their own?

Mentally shrugging, Jane focused her attention back on Grace. It was not like she would ever allow Grace and her brother to suffer. Between herself, Elizabeth, and William, she knew provisions would be made for the children's future care. What concerned her at the moment was the heat coming off the little girl in her arms.

"Grace, how are you feeling this morning?" Jane asked while smoothed Grace's hair back from her face.

"Mmm...fuzzy." Grace sighed and rubbed at her chest before saying, "I will be fine. I can still help you take care of Allen."

Brow furrowed in concern, Jane asked, "Do you hurt anywhere, Grace?"

Grace seemed to sigh again, then rubbing her forehead, she said, "Yes."

Jane did not like the floaty way Grace sounded when she spoke. Grace had definitely caught whatever had befallen her family. Pressing her lips together, Jane looked down at the sleeping Allen. The boy seemed to sleep deeply. Reaching out, she placed her hand on his forehead. While he was warm, he was not nearly as hot as his sister and had improved from the night before.

Kissing the top of Grace's head, Jane asked, "Grace, I want to move you to the big bed your parents used. I think you and your brother would be much more comfortable."

Grace sleepily nuzzled her head into Jane's body, and after a moment, she mumbled, "All right."

It was not the easiest thing for Jane to stand with her arms full of the seven-year-old, but she managed to take Grace to bed and tuck her in. It was much easier to pick up Allen's much smaller form and transfer him to the bed. In this way, she could sit in the chair next to the bed, and the children might be able to get some well-needed rest.

IT DID NOT TAKE long for Jane's worst fears to come to fruition. Grace's fever grew worse as the night progressed. By morning, Jane knew that Allen was on the path to recovery. She also knew that if things did not improve, she might very well lose Grace.

When Grace started coughing, Jane forced her tired body to move. She would need steam and more of the liniment if she was going to keep the cough from settling deep in Grace's chest. Leaving the room, Jane went out into the kitchen where there was a kettle on the stove. Pouring boiling water into a bowl, she brought it back and placed it on the small table next to the bed. Aiding her to sit up, she held Grace over the bowl and helped her to breathe the vapor with a towel draped over the young girl's head. Jane knew that the steam somehow helped loosen the mucus in her chest.

Even when the coughing finally settled, Grace's troubles did not go away. She seemed to dream or possibly hallucinate. Crying out to her brother, she said, "Allen, don't cry. I will take care of you even if mama's sleeping. Don't cry."

Jane's heart went out to the poor girl who, even in her delusions, sought to care for the one family member she had left. Sitting on the bed, Jane pulled Grace to herself, rocking her and soothing her brow with a cool compress. She murmured, "Shhh, Grace. Your brother is fine, he is well. Do not worry."

"What is wrong with her, Miss Jane?" Looking over, Jane saw Allen's wide, worried eyes staring at his feverish sister.

Plastering a smile on her tired face, Jane said, "Your sister is just talking in her sleep. Do not worry, I am taking care of her."

Allen's expression was too knowing for a child so young, but he had just recently witnessed the loss of most of his family. Shaking his little head, he said, "She is sick now too, isn't she?"

"Yes, but you are better. I am sure that she will get better soon enough." Jane hoped she was not lying to the poor boy. "Are you hungry or thirsty, Allen?"

Sitting up in bed, he grinned. "Yeah."

Lying Grace back down on the bed, Jane tucked her in and smiled at the boy. It was a good sign that his appetite was returning. Removing the rag from Grace's forehead, she swirled it around in the bowl with cool vinegar water before wringing it out and placing it back on Grace's head. "I will go and look in the kitchen and see what I can get you to eat. Will you watch over your sister while I am gone?"

Allen sat up a little straighter, as if proud to have been given a task. "Yes, I can do that."

Leaning over, she ruffled his damp hair and said, "You are such a good brother. Just call out if you need my help. I will be quick."

Leaving the room, Jane waited until the door was closed behind her to stretch out her neck and back. Leaning over the children and spending most of the day and night in the wooden chair was not helping her posture. At least she did not seem to be becoming ill.

Going over to the small table she had set up with water and strong soft soap, she began scrubbing at her hands up past her wrists. Her mother had sent a batch of their most powerful soap for people, promising to wash away any dirt or grime and hopefully illness. Jane's grandmother had always insisted that cleanliness was next to godliness. The journals had often pointed out that strict hygiene seemed to prevent the spread of illness. The compassionate words she discovered in those journals had deeply moved Jane, motivating her to extend her care to the sick and those in need.

Turning to the kitchen, Jane spotted Susan at the table folding the linens that she had laundered. "Do we still have some of the broth? Allen is awake and has asked for something to eat."

Standing, Susan hurried to the table, her excitement at the news evident at the energy in her step and the tone of her voice when she said, "I am glad. You said that you thought he would recover, and it seems he is." Ladling out a cup of broth, she poured it in a mug before adding, "After being unwell for so long, I thought a mug might be better than a bowl for the lad. Here, you take a roll as well. You need to keep your strength up, too. I can't have you getting ill." Handing the mug to Jane, she turned and grabbed a dinner roll off the plate on the kitchen table and handed that to her as well.

"Thank you for looking after me, Susan," Jane said gratefully as she took a small bite of the roll, savoring the buttery soft texture and rich flavor. It seemed to be the best roll she had ever tasted; that or she was exceedingly tired and hungry. It was possible she was hungry, tired, and it was the best ever roll. Her own inner dialogue had Jane rolling her eyes at her antics. Maybe she needed to take a break and rest after all.

Going back to the table, Susan picked up a sheet from a pile. "How is young Grace?"

Shaking her head, Jane sighed and answered, "Not well at all. Her fever is staying quite high, and she has developed a cough." Jane squared her shoulders. She would rest after Grace improved or her fever at least broke. "Thank you for the roll and the broth for Allen and, of course, for all of your hard work with all the household chores."

Returning to Allen, she inelegantly shoved what was left of the roll in her mouth and chewed and swallowed hurriedly. Brushing crumbs from her mouth with her free hand, she smiled and then opened the door. It would not do to let Allen know how weary she was.

Chapter Ten

Bingley's mind was too full of his questions about the future, and he had been unable to sleep the night before. Getting out of bed, he stood at his window watching the sunrise paint the landscape with colors. First, purples chased away the gray and then pink dotted the landscape. By the time that peach and yellow joined the dance, immersing the world in a morning glow, he had saddled his horse and headed out.

Unanswered and unasked questions weighed heavily on Bingley's mind, urging him to find the courage to speak. He knew he would only find the happiness he sought with Jane by his side. However, she would only be by his side if he asked her to stay there. He had known for some time that he loved Jane. He longed for her to be his wife, and he now admitted to himself that only his cowardice was currently keeping them apart. That and an epidemic.

Soon enough, Bingley walked into the McGregors' silent house. He immediately stoked the fire in the fireplace and restarted the fire in the stove. He had been assisting enough to know that they would need both throughout the day. Bingley wanted to help however he could. With Grace falling ill, Jane and Susan were increasingly fatigued as they worked tirelessly to care for the sick children.

Walking softly, he moved to the room that housed the two remaining McGregors. Bingley opened the door, seeking out Jane in the dim room. She sat in a chair by the bed, slumped over, her hand resting on Grace. Shaking his head, Bingley sighed. She would never get enough rest in that fashion and would likely fall ill herself.

He would support her in caring for those in need, but he was unwilling to watch her undermine her own health. A few quiet steps took him as far as the bed, and he gazed down at both of the children who had suffered so much, losing almost all of their family, and then becoming so sick themselves. Allen lay on his back with his arms and legs spread wide, taking up as much space as possible. The flush of fever had left him, and he appeared to be sleeping peacefully. His older sister Grace was curled on her side, almost clinging to Jane, and was it any wonder? Jane had been a lifeline for the girl, mothering and helping her at a time when it must have seemed that her world was ending.

Bingley leaned over, checking both children's temperatures. Allen was indeed free of fever, and his breaths seemed to be easy and unlabored. Grace was warm, but the blazing fire that had consumed her for the last day or so had finally receded. Satisfied with the results, Bingley turned his attention towards Jane.

She was quite disheveled, and yet all he could see was her beauty. Her blonde hair was tangled and lank, coming out of a braid that hung down her back. The blue eyes that he loved so much were hidden, sheltered behind pale lids and dark lashes. It was easy to discern how tired she was, even in her sleep. Dark circles were prominent in her pale face. Her pink cupid's bow lips were turned down in sleep. It was odd watching her frown in her sleep. Jane was always smiling, except apparently when asleep.

Of course, he was aware of how much the smile was a mask that she hid behind, especially when unhappy or worried. She genuinely smiled when she was happy, and she often was happy, but it was only then that her smile traveled from her lips to her eyes. He loved it when her eyes sparkled with joy. He was, however, very fascinated by her down-turned lips, so rarely seen.

He stepped closer to Jane, untangling her hand from Grace's ever so slowly to avoid waking them both. Once she was free, he carefully scooped her up, carrying her like the precious cargo that she was. He brought her to the next room, where she had not been spending enough time sleeping.

Her not waking told him all he needed to know about how exhausted she was. Only once he had placed her in the bed did he notice Susan was not asleep on the pallet on the floor like he had assumed. She lay there watching him with a wide grin.

Figuring he should say something, he whispered, "She needs her rest, and I do not mind caring for the children."

Nodding her head, her eyes dancing, Susan said, "She has been working too hard. I will get up and start tea and breakfast once I dress."

Realizing that he was in the way, he glanced back at Jane briefly before leaving the room so that the maid could dress and begin her day. Walking out into the kitchen, Bingley pulled the door shut behind him. It was easy to see that the fire in the fireplace and stove were both progressing nicely. They had plenty of firewood, as James had come by the day before and chopped a surplus of firewood for their use.

Going out to the little yard, Bingley drew some water. It was a task he had grown accustomed to only in the recent week of struggle. Bringing the water in, he looked around, trying to decide how to best be useful. Only when he could find nothing else to do and Susan had begun bustling about, he went out to retrieve the book he had left in his saddlebag.

Moving into the room where the children slept, Bingley sat down and read. *Gulliver's Travels* was a book he had read before, but he found it entertaining and, should the children wake, he figured they might find it entertaining. Though not as widely read as Darcy, he enjoyed passing the time with a good book when the occasion called for it.

JANE WOKE UP ALL at once and was completely confused. She was certain that she had been with Grace and Allen tending to Grace's high fever, and yet she was in the little bed, tucked in quite nicely with her shoes removed. Glancing around the room, she found herself alone. Making herself move and get on her feet, Jane shuffled out of the room and into the kitchen, following the smell of cooking.

"Did you sleep well, Miss Bennet?" Susan asked from where she stood stirring the pot on the stove.

"Yes, I think I did, though I am slightly confused. What time is it?" Covering a prodigious yawn, Jane looked out the window.

Holding up a bowl, Susan replied, "Midafternoon. I have a pot of soup on if you are hungry."

"Yes, thank you. It smells lovely." Sitting at the table, Jane watched as Susan ladled up some soup. Jane rubbed her eyes, still feeling disoriented. She assumed the children were well. The last she remembered was Grace's fever finally breaking. As she watched Grace fall into a peaceful slumber, a sense of relief had washed over her. Then she woke up in bed. What exactly had happened? "I do not remember lying down."

Placing a bowl of soup before her with a spoon, Susan said, "That would be because Mr. Bingley put you to bed, miss." Susan smiled at Jane as she spoke, though a pink blush appeared on her cheeks. "It was right romantic if I do say so, miss. Not that I would ever say anything about it to anyone."

Running her hand down her face, Jane wondered if she should be flattered or horribly embarrassed. Possibly both? "He did?" She would not worry about anything to do with a compromise. She had worked closely enough with Susan to know that it was not something she needed to fret over.

Nodding her head, Susan's blush turned darker. "Yes, miss. He was anxious about you. I believe you have found yourself excellent husband material in that man."

"You know, you may be right." Fighting her own blush, Jane took a bite of the rich soup. Chewing slowly, she swallowed before saying, "Are the children sleeping?"

"Maybe, I do not know. The last time I checked, Mr. Bingley was reading to them."

Choking in surprise, Jane swallowed carefully and regained her composure before she looked up at Susan, her eyes watering. "Reading to them?"

Nodding, Susan grinned. "Oh yes, all of them seemed to be enjoying it, too."

Jane looked over her shoulder in the direction of the room he and the children were in.

Susan seemed to catch Jane's thoughts because she laughed and said, "You finish your soup while it is warm, miss. You can go in and see them soon enough."

Though Jane was sure that the soup was most likely delicious, she did not taste a thing in her rush to eat and go check on Charles and the children. Her mind must still be sleep addled because it had taken a moment for her to process that Susan had said both children were enjoying being read to. Had Grace improved that much?

Rising, Jane took her now empty bowl and placed it in the tub that Susan had been using for dirty dishes and thanked her for the meal. Jane heard Susan chuckle as she left the kitchen and went to check on the children. Yes, she told herself, it was the children she was rushing to see. It wasn't the man who had been caring for them so that she could sleep. Opening the door, Jane could not stop the pounding in her heart when she saw Charles sitting on the chair beside the bed. He was reading, but when Allen stirred in his sleep, Charles reached out and settled the blanket more firmly around the slight form.

Jane must have made a sound because Charles looked up at her and placed his finger in the book to mark his page. "They are sleeping, but both of them seem to be doing much better."

THEY STARED AT EACH other for a moment, and the air seemed to hang heavy with anticipation. Jane's eyes locked with Charles's, and in that moment, she saw the depth of his character and recognized what a truly wonderful man he was. He had come to help, spending his time bringing joy to sick orphans. Then too she couldn't forget the way he carried her to bed and lovingly tucked her in when she was too exhausted to do it herself. What was holding her back any longer? Jane's hesitation felt misplaced, as he had more than proven himself.

It seemed, however, that Charles's mind was on less existential issues because he blurted, "You are so beautiful."

Startled at his declaration, Jane looked at Charles with wide eyes. She knew she must look a fright. She had not even considered brushing out her hair in days; it was a tangled mess half hanging out of a simple braid. Her clothes were rumpled and wrinkled after being slept in, and Jane was sure she must have dark circles under her eyes. What could he be thinking of? Shaking her head, Jane said, "Beautiful? I know I am a mess. You must be more sleep deprived than I am."

Shaking his head, Charles said, "Don't you know by now that when I speak of your beauty, it is not only your appearance that I speak of? It does not matter what you wear or how your hair is arranged; to me, your beauty comes from who you are, the kindness you demonstrate to the world around you. You are to your core, beautiful." Leaning forward in his chair, Charles gripped her hand. "You could have so easily closed off your heart to the world after the childhood that you experienced, but you did not. You pushed forward, always willing to help others, endeavoring to see to it that others are happy. You are caring for these children as if they were your own, not because you will benefit, but because they will. That is what I consider beautiful."

Jane could not have been more startled if Charles had declared that he wanted to move to Australia and live with kangaroos. How had she not realized he had felt this way? He had often spoken of her beauty, but when he realized that she was not particularly fond of the word, he had stopped. Had he been speaking of this the whole time? Finding it difficult to master her voice, Jane whispered, "I did not know. I did not understand."

Charles's hand went to Jane's face, tracing a delicate brow with a trembling finger. Then, after sliding down along her cheek, he cupped her face, saying, "I know that you have been bombarded by your *beauty* for years. You have been pursued by men who use the word as if it were a prize, men who would use your physical beauty as an adornment for themselves. There are those who foolishly only see the surface of your beauty and merely see your superficial smile. Meanwhile, your goodness, your kindness, your true beauty glimmers from your very being, and can be seen by those who choose to see it."

Blinking back tears, Jane said, "I never thought I would ever see the day when someone beyond my sisters could see through my mask."

"I know you hide behind a facade to protect yourself, but it is more fragile than you know. I can see the effort you put into wearing it and how it affects you. Do not misunderstand me—your mask is matchless, but your beauty and smiles while lovely do not always represent your genuine feelings." Leaning down, he laid his forehead against hers, continuing under his breath, "It is the real you I love, not your so-called *beauty*, not the smile you feel you must show the world."

"You are an aggravating man for telling me this at such a time." Jane rested her forehead against Charles, breathing in his scent and letting all that he was soak into her heart. Giving a soft laugh, she said, "What am I to do with your love now? When we are both too busy caring for others to rejoice as we would wish?"

Pulling back, Charles looked into her eyes and said, "You can agree to love me as I have long loved you, for nothing less than forever.

Agree to marry me as soon as we are free to hear the banns read. Agree to be my wife."

Throwing her arms around Charles, she nearly forgot herself in her joy, but at the last moment she remembered the sleeping children and nodded her head before whispering, "Yes!"

How had such sorrow and loss led her to such a place of happiness and joy? She no longer had any doubt about his motives or the depth of his affection for her. Just as a steady drip of water erodes stone, his unwavering love and steadfast demeanor had gradually eroded her fears and doubts.

Jane's lips met his in a tender embrace, and the world around them seemed to fade away. It was so intoxicating that Jane momentarily forgot about everything else until Grace's small giggle broke the spell and brought them back to reality. For a moment, Jane was captivated by the warmth in Charles's smiling eyes, but then she forced herself to look over and check on Grace.

"You look at each other the way Mama and Papa did." She rubbed at her eye, a soft smile spreading across her face as she looked up at Charles and Jane in their embrace.

Jane gazed down at Grace, happy despite the interruption. Leaving Charles's side, she leaned over and felt Grace's brow, and was glad to find her cool to the touch. "How are you feeling, my dear?"

"Much better," Grace said with a contented sigh.

BINGLEY LOOKED DOWN INTO the sleepy eyes of the child he and Jane had both worried so much about. There was a light in her eyes that had been missing the last few days. While that was encouraging, it was the statement she had made that he could not stop pondering.

He marveled at how a seven-year-old girl was able to recognize the love that he shared with Jane. She did not know their entire story, but she had recognized something in their look that reminded her of a happily married couple who she loved. Letting the melody of Jane's conversation with the little girl wash over him, he basked in the moment's joy. Elation was hardly a strong enough word to adequately describe what he felt at finally knowing that Jane had gifted him with her love and trust.

Turning his attention outward, Bingley watched Jane and Grace talk softly. The tired lines around her eyes were less noticeable than they had been, but they were still present. Even after having rested, she still appeared worn. Bingley also saw that she had dropped her mask, and she wore a naturally joyous smile. Clearly, Jane was delighted with the girl's rapid improvement. Jane looked so relieved, and that in itself lightened his heart.

He began paying more attention to the conversation when he heard Jane say, "We can't have you wasting away without something to eat. Would you like some broth and perhaps a roll?"

Grace's eyes lit up. Her expressive smile was a wonderful contrast to how listless she had been only the day before. "Yes, please!"

Bingley stood and helping Jane to her feet, he moved with her to the door. They walked into the kitchen, where they found Susan chopping carrots at the table and humming under her breath.

"Miss Grace has asked for some broth and bread," Jane said, her voice dancing as she finished washing her hands. Bingley started washing his own hands with the soap, happy to hear the joy in Jane's voice.

"Oh, that is splendid." Hopping up from her seat, Susan rushed to the stove where she had been keeping broth simmering in case it was needed. She ladled out some of the broth and scooped up one of the many rolls she seemed to be making regularly. She handed them over with a wide smile. "I have been praying that she would show signs of recovery."

"I think we all have," Jane said, her voice soft and almost reverent.

It was quiet in the kitchen for a while, and Bingley wondered if Jane and Susan were also thinking of how close they had come to losing Allen and Grace, or how they had lost all the other members of the small family. Hating to think that their jovial mood was about to disappear, Bingley searched for something to say. He knew that something in the kitchen smelled amazing, so he asked, "Something smells splendid, Susan, and I do not think it is the broth. What are you making?"

Susan blushed and waved her hand in the air in an embarrassed manner before saying, "I'm just making some stew. I thought we might be needing something heartier given how tired we all are. Then too with the children improving, I thought it would be a good idea to provide something more nourishing."

Bingley smiled in response, grateful for such a thoughtful meal because despite the grave circumstances, they had much to be thankful for.

Chapter Eleven

Jane watched as they drew closer to Pemberley and could not but help feel that it had been an age and a half since she had seen the estate. Had it only been a fortnight? It had seemed longer.

She had dealt with death and celebrated life. Jane had even let Charles into her heart the way she should have long ago. She would have thought that having someone take a place in her heart would have felt heavy, but it was nothing like that.

While it had been a struggle to let go enough to give Charles a place in her heart, doing so had been a release of sorts. Instead of feeling burdened, she found that having another person to love lifted her spirits and made her feel buoyant.

Glancing over, Jane could see Charles as he rode beside the wagon. As if feeling her eyes on him, he glanced up and smiled. "Are you happy to be making your way back home?"

Smiling back, she said, "Yes, I will be happy to see my sisters. I know they will have worried for me this whole time."

His earnest blue eyes scanned her as she sat next to the driver, then he said, "I will be happy when you can get a full night's sleep without waking up to care for others. You need to care only for yourself for a time."

Jane wrinkled her nose. She was not that tired. "I am hardier than I look, Charles. I am well enough."

"You may be well enough for you, but not for me, nor would I guess your mother and sisters." Allowing his horse its head, he locked gazes with her and said, "I love your determination, but you are drooping. Your eyes seem bruised, and your hands are cracked from so much time spent washing them with the strong soap. Most of all, your heart still aches from losing four of the McGregors. I know that saving Grace and Allen doesn't erase that pain for you. You need rest and the comfort your mother and sisters will provide. If you want to appear tolerable at our wedding, it's important that you rest beforehand."

Jane's mind went back to the morning that felt so long ago when she made the leap to tell him that she did not like being called beautiful. He had asked if he should call her tolerable instead. Knowing that he was thinking of that time as well made her smile. He was not wrong, of course, but she playfully added, "You could see all that."

She watched him carefully and, in doing so, she saw how hard he was trying to keep a straight face. He was not very convincing, because his lips kept twitching at the corners. "Yes," he responded.

"Tolerable indeed," Jane managed to say without laughing, though she did give in and rolled her eyes.

Elizabeth rushed through the house, excited to know that her sister would be returning home. Though she knew her sister was well enough, she still desperately wanted to lay eyes on Jane herself.

Being separated from Jane at such a time had cut like a knife. Not only did she want to talk about her impending motherhood with her, but she suspected that Jane would have her own stories to tell. She and Bingley had been getting closer to the point of something before everything started going bad. As close as they had been working together, Elizabeth was almost certain they would have come to an understanding by now.

She grumbled at herself as she hurried down the last hall and towards the front windows. She had every intention of rising early and seeing to everything so that she could greet Jane when she arrived, but she had again slept late. William refused to wake her and had told her lady's maid to let her sleep. He insisted she must need the extra rest and was not about to disturb that and risk hurting her or the baby.

The dear man was always looking out for her, and she loved him for it, but still it was frustrating. At least she was not ill, as were some of the expectant mothers she had encountered. That was a blessing.

She rather detested being sick. She would take sleepy over nauseous any day.

Skidding to a halt, Elizabeth narrowly missed running into Lydia. Elizabeth and Lydia locked gazes, and in an instant, the hall was filled with their joyous laughter. Linking arms with her younger but recently taller sister, Elizabeth managed to contain her giggles as long as she did not look Lydia in the eye. They were most alike of all their sisters. Only Elizabeth normally contained herself a little more than Lydia, though sometimes her wit and humor shone through.

Moving in unison, they continued at a more leisurely pace. They eagerly anticipated the arrival of their absent sister. Elizabeth sobered slightly, realizing that she had been so focused on the stress of caring for Pemberley and everything else that she had not thought at all about how worried Lydia must have been. She had been so wrapped up in concern for the tenants and her pregnancy that she had spared little thought to how her sisters had been bearing up under their own worries.

"Did you sleep in again?" Lydia asked, a playful edge in her lyrical voice. Elizabeth relaxed slightly, knowing that her sister held nothing against her.

Elizabeth rolled her eyes at her new sleep habit. She had always been one to wake early enough to greet the sun, but that had changed with her pregnancy. Grumbling slightly, Elizabeth said, "Yes, and that silly husband of mine insisted I must need the extra rest, or else I would have woken up on my own. He does not have to rush around seeing to things in less time than before. I had a system to my day, you know!"

Squeezing her sister's arm as they walked, Lydia said, "The nerve of him wanting the best for you and your growing child!"

Elizabeth huffed and then tilted her nose into an air, assuming the air of injured dignity. "Indeed!" At that point, Elizabeth and Lydia made the mistake of catching each other's glance again, and both dissolved into peals of laughter.

Lydia's interactions with her were a balm of sorts. Elizabeth didn't begrudge her sisters the eventual life and love that she knew they would all find. Every one of them deserved to find a love as wonderful as what she had with William. She was slightly sad because in the center of her being, Elizabeth knew she would soon lose Jane to her own life and love. Smiling, Elizabeth pulled Lydia a little closer to her side. It was nice to know she still had several years with Lydia before she lost her, as well.

SLIDING OFF HIS HORSE, Bingley hurried to Jane's side to help her down from the wagon. He had thought of arranging for her to ride back to Pemberley in a carriage, but Jane had balked at the idea, insisting that the wagon was bringing back supplies and Susan, anyway. Why should she require a second conveyance?

Who was he to say otherwise? So here he was, escorting her back to her family. Her all-consuming smile told him how much she was eagerly anticipating seeing her mother and sisters. It was her genuine smile, not her mask. Bingley freely admitted to himself that he would do anything to keep that lovely smile on her face.

He had already crossed off all but the closest estates that he had looked at. He knew Jane could never live very far from her sisters and mother. The estate he had visited a while back on the other side of Kympton might meet with approval. It was not Pemberley's equal, but neither he nor Jane cared for extravagance.

Bingley clasped Jane around the waist and lifted her to the ground without kissing her, but it was a near thing. It did not help that the way Jane wrapped her arm around his offered elbow and leaned into him as they walked up the path to the house was unmistakably possessive, not to mention distracting.

They were within fifteen feet of the side door when the squealing started. Giving her arm one last squeeze before stepping back, he watched as Jane was enveloped by a plethora of dress-clad bodies.

For a moment, Bingley could not decipher all the overlapping conversations, but eventually he heard Mrs. Bennet say, "Stand back and let me get a look at you." Mrs. Bennet took her daughter by the shoulders, studying her as only a mother could. She clucked under her breath when she noticed what Bingley had already seen. It had been a long, hard week for Jane. "You are going to take the next few days to rest, young lady. Good food, naps, and time with us all is what you need."

When Jane seemed about to protest, Elizabeth linked arms with her and guided her in the direction of the house, saying. "Do not fret,

Jane, you can join me. I have no energy lately and keep sleeping in."
All the sisters closed rank around the two, fluttering around like so
many butterflies.

Moving to follow them into the house, a hand on his elbow
stopped Bingley. Looking down, he saw Mrs. Bennet standing there.
She was mostly composed, but upon seeing the moisture in her eyes,
he asked, "Mrs. Bennet, are you well?"

FANNY BENNET STUDIED THE man who she knew had taken hold
of her oldest daughter's heart. She had long known that it would
take a special man to see through her daughter's hard-earned defenses
and find a way in. She had worried Jane might never open herself to
anyone besides her trusted sisters.

Mr. Bingley had been a support to her and her girls for a while
now. He had been there when they attained their freedom from her
wretched husband. He had helped his friend William during the
recent distress with all the sick tenants, willingly risking his health to
assist others. It was clear that he was a man quite unlike many others.

Most important to Fanny was the way he looked at her daughter,
as if she was his next breath, as if he could not breathe if he could
not see her. Above all else, she wanted that for her girls. That kind
of love would see them through nearly anything. Oh, there would be
problems, but if they worked together, they could make it through
the problems the world was sure to throw at them.

When it seemed that Mr. Bingley was confused by her stare, his eyebrows having crawled up into his hairline, Fanny finally said, "Thank you for watching out for my girl. I know my daughter. She would have easily pushed herself straight past exhaustion without someone there to rein her in."

Nodding, the young man pursed his lips and then drew closer, enveloping her in a hug as he whispered, "Always. I will always watch out for her." Then, after a heartbeat, he said, "And all those that she loves. You and your daughters will always have a place with us should you need it."

Fanny's throat was too clogged with emotion to say anything for a moment. She could only look at the dear man with love in his eyes. Jane had chosen well. Taking a deep breath, she pushed back her maudlin thoughts and asked, "So, have you set a date yet?"

Laughing out loud, he paused to catch his breath before saying, "Mothers always know," with a smile on his face. Offering her his arm, he began walking with her into the grand house that was Pemberley. Patting her hand where it rested on his arm, he added, "We have not."

Smiling at him, she replied, "It will only take three weeks to read the banns, and I find that I am quite fond of the idea of lots of grandchildren."

The laugh that she elicited with her comment made everyone stare at him as they entered the morning room.

Offering the group an unapologetic look, he pointed at his future mother-in-law and said, "Your mother has given me her blessing and has requested a lot of grandchildren."

While Jane looked slightly mortified, it was Lydia who laughed, saying, "Mother! You have five daughters. I am sure between us you will have plenty of babies to coddle. Do not make Jane think she has to have all of them!"

Smiling at her youngest, Fanny tilted her head, and with her best mother's voice said, "Yes dear, I am sure that if your sisters lag behind, you will shore up the numbers." Lydia's huff set everyone laughing.

Epilogue

"BUT WHAT ABOUT THE children? You said that they were better, but surely you could not have left them all alone! All of their family was dead!" Evaline could not keep the concern from her voice and knew her eyebrows had risen into her hairline.

Despite her raised voice, Jane simply offered her a kind smile. "They had an aunt and uncle living in Kympton. Unaffected by the sickness, Mr. and Mrs. Wright hurriedly traveled to Pemberley upon hearing of the McGregor family's dire situation." Looking up at her husband, she smiled at him in a soft way that Evaline did not quite understand before looking back at her. "We would have taken in the children ourselves had the Wrights not been so happy to have Grace and Allen in their lives. They had desperately desired to have children for years, and despite the tragedy of Mrs. Wright losing her younger sister and most of their family, they saw Grace and Allen as a blessing in their lives."

Nestling back into her chair, Evaline attempted to settle her heart. Even at twelve, Evaline found it difficult to comprehend how difficult it would be to lose both her parents in such a horrible way. How was Grace able to bear it at seven? How was she able to bear any of it? The sickness, the death, caring for her younger brother before help arrived?

Tilting her head, Evaline tried to look at the bright side of things. At least Grace and Allen were able to settle into a nice home with their aunt and uncle. Though they had lost their parents, they still had people who loved them. Looking back at Jane and Mr. Bingley, she managed a smile. "It is wonderful they all ended up happy together."

"Yes, I am happy they all got the family they needed," Jane agreed from where she sat, leaning into her husband. "I visit them whenever possible. They live in the town of Kympton, above their aunt and uncle's bakery. Both children seem to be thriving in their new situation, despite everything that they experienced."

Looking around the room at the three couples, Evaline grinned. "Am I imagining it, or do you sisters tend to come to the love of your lives in the most interesting ways?"

From where she sat across from her husband at the chessboard, Elizabeth laughed. "Yes, it seems we do, but you must admit that despite the trouble we go through, we end up with the best of men." Leaning over the table, Mr. Darcy blatantly kissed his wife. Evaline found herself looking away from such obvious evidence of their love until she heard Elizabeth say, "Do not think that kiss is distracting me. You are still in check."

Mr. Darcy smiled, showing off his dimples before responding with, "Yes, I see that, my love."

Soon after that, Evaline made her way up to the bed that awaited her. She was better, but still tired easily since she had been so sick after the blizzard. With the aid of a maid, she readied for bed, feeling the warmth of the sheets envelope her as she prepared to fall into a peaceful slumber. Oddly enough, as she drifted off to sleep, she found herself thinking about Lydia. She was the only Bennet sister who had not found her match yet. She had never met the girl but based on how each of her sisters had found happiness, she wondered what kind of adventure Lydia would have on her way to true love.

Acknowledgements

Before you go, I'd like to express my gratitude to all those who assisted me in bringing the Bennet sisters' stories to the world. I'd like to start by acknowledging and thanking the people closest to me. It was thanks to my sister Megan's encouragement that I began writing. Then there is my mother, who serves as my alpha reader and sounding board for fresh ideas. My sister Chelsea's support is invaluable, just like the inspiration I find in my nieces and nephew for my younger characters. If you haven't had the pleasure of debating with a one-year-old who can articulate their thoughts in complete sentences, you're missing out. It is an absolute delight!

Additionally, I would like to extend my appreciation to my Beta readers and the people who show support through my newsletter. Doris, Debra, Carol, and Frankie, working with you to bring my stories to the world has been an honor. The encouragement and feedback I get from you helps me more than you know.

Lastly, it has been an utter pleasure working with my editor, Tayler. Your feedback not only helps me ensure that my story flows and my characters shine, but I also thoroughly enjoy reading your comments. I always love seeing your emojis in the comments, especially the ones with heart eyes!

Most importantly, I would like to thank you. It's been a joy to create this work of love, but without readers, it would be an exercise in futility. The fact that you chose my book to read is an honor. Thank you for taking the time to finish my book, I hope the characters and their stories resonated with you.

If you enjoyed reading this book, please consider leaving an honest review on your favorite site. It does not have to be very long, but I would really appreciate the feedback.

About the Author

MY JOURNEY WITH WORDS started out as a painful one. The letters on the page seemed to taunt me, and I spent countless hours with my mother trying to decipher their meaning. Our reading journey started with Little House on the Prairie and continued with other books, mostly in the historical fiction genre. Slowly but surely, I started reading independently, advancing from historical fiction to fantasy and science fiction.

The stories I found in the books I read held me captive, and I often lost track of time. The realization of the true power of the written word inspired me to pursue writing. Unfortunately, I had to put it on the back burner in order to deal with pesky things like paying for food and housing. Then a dare from my sister brought back memories of my passion for writing in high school. It was a passion that I was determined to rekindle.

When I got back into writing, I turned to my latest reading addiction for inspiration, Pride and Prejudice Variations. My mind was fixated on the regency era and the romance of Elizabeth and

Darcy, making it hard to write anything else. So I went with it and here we are.

Visit jaimemariewrites.com to delve into my world of words, or find me on Instagram @jaimemariewrites for a glimpse into my creative process.

Books by Jaime Marie Lang

The Bennet Ladies Liberation Series

Darcy's Gallant Gambit

Kitty Catches Kismet

Mary's Daring Demand

Jane's Fragile Façade

Lydia Acquires Adoration

Other Novels

Murdered on a Wednesday: A Pride and Prejudice Mystery